NO WAY OUT!

Jessie lost sight of Ki when gunfire from the three highwaymen forced her out of the saddle and down to the ground, where she took cover behind one of the boulders. With her back pressed up against it, she thumbed cartridges out of her cartridge belt loops and loaded the empty chambers of her gun's cylinder. Then turning around again, she was startled to see three other riders heading in her direction. They were too far away for her to recognize them at first, but then, as they came closer, she saw with an odd mixture of relief and apprehension that the riders were Mel Bronson, Jim Bob Simpson and Charles Proctor.

Vigilantes . . . !

→•← WESLEY ELLIS →•←

LONE STAR

AND THE
DEADLY VIGILANTES

J

JOVE BOOKS, NEW YORK

LONE STAR AND THE DEADLY VIGILANTES

A Jove Book / published by arrangement with
the author

PRINTING HISTORY
Jove edition / November 1991

ISBN: 0-515-10709-3

★

Chapter 1

"Come on, Ki!" Jessie Starbuck cried, taking her friend's hand and trying to draw him closer to the ticket booth that was painted peppermint red and white.

"Jessie, if the Good Lord had wanted me to fly, he would have given me wings. I'm not going up in that hot-air balloon, not for a million dollars. What would happen if it sprung a leak while we're way up there in the middle of the air?"

"It's perfectly safe," Jessie insisted. "See? It says so right there on that sign."

Ki glanced at the sign Jessie had pointed out, which read: "Safe for all. Bring the kiddies and ride high above the earth in Professor Bixby's Hot Air Balloon. See the sights. Then tell your friends about your great adventure!"

"You go ahead if you want to, Jessie," he said, backing away. "I'll stay down here on terra firma while you go up among the heavenly hosts."

"Ki, I'm surprised at you, My brave and fearless friend is afraid to go up in a hot-air balloon? I can't believe it."

"Believe it."

1

"Step right up, ladies and gents," a top-hatted man with a waxed and curled black mustache cried from the ticket booth in front of the tethered balloon, which was gaudily painted with purple polka dots and red stars. "I, Professor Bixby, will send you on a tour of the countryside from the vantage point of my remarkable conveyance. Only one dollar for adults and half that small price for the youngsters. Who'll be the first to step right up and—"

"We will," Jessie interrupted, practically dragging Ki up to the professor and holding out two dollars.

"Jessie," Ki said, "I don't—"

"We want two tickets to ride," Jessie said firmly, silencing Ki with a stern glance.

Professor Bixby snatched the two dollars out of Jessie's hand as if he were afraid to give her and Ki time to change their minds. "Step right up here on this platform, *mademoiselle*," he said with a quick twirl of his mustache. "That's it. Now step into the gondola. Very good. Now you, sir."

Ki was about to decline the invitation when Jessie pulled and Professor Bixby pushed and he found himself standing inside the wicker basket beside Jessie.

"Now then," cried Professor Bixby, pocketing the two dollars, "who's next? We have limited space, as you can see, ladies and gents, so step right up and don't miss out on this opportunity of a lifetime."

Jessie and Ki made room for a young man of no more than sixteen wearing a straw hat and bib overalls who was grinning from ear to ear as he took his place in the basket.

"He's not afraid," Jessie whispered to Ki.

"I didn't say I was afraid. I just said I don't think people were meant to go gallivanting through the sky in a contraption like this one."

Jessie smiled to herself as Professor Bixby continued trying to sell tickets but found no more takers.

She was a tall woman, but in no way ungainly. Her wavy copper-colored hair caught and reflected the bright sunlight that flooded down on the dusty county fairgrounds. It reached her shoulders and gracefully haloed her face. She had bright green eyes set like two limpid emeralds beneath her smooth brow. Her figure was full in the right places, slender everywhere else.

Beside her, Ki was a contrast in many ways. His hair, worn shoulder length, was black and straight. His skin, not as smooth as Jessie's, was of a color that hinted at his Oriental heritage, as did his slightly slanted eyes. Born of a Japanese woman and sired by an American sailor in Japan, he had, once grown, come to work for Alex Starbuck, Jessie's late father, and in time had arrived in America with his employer to take on the task of serving as companion and confidant to Alex Starbuck's young and lovely daughter.

As the years passed, their companionship became friendship, and a bond grew between them that was by now unbreakable. It was a bond formed of mutual affection and respect. Ki could no more imagine a life without Jessie now than Jessie herself could imagine living alone without her friend of many years.

"No more takers?" a somewhat disappointed and disgruntled Professor Bixby asked, surveying the crowd with what was more a sneer than a smile on his lips. "Well, perhaps next trip you'll want to go, ladies and gents. Especially when you hear the enthusiastic reports of these three passengers once they have returned from the wondrous vault of the sky to our mundane earth."

"*If* we return," Ki muttered, and was promptly hushed by Jessie.

Professor Bixby signaled to his assistant, a man with a bulbous red-veined nose, and the man promptly stoked the fire that fed hot air into the balloon towering overhead.

At the same time, Professor Bixby detached several heavy bags of sand that had been tied to the gondola beneath the balloon. His action caused the balloon to rise several inches off the ground, and Ki exclaimed, "Let me out of here!"

Too late.

The balloon rose swiftly up into the air, the gondola below it swaying slightly.

"Look!" an excited Jessie cried, pointing to the horizon now clearly visible in the distance.

3

But Ki wasn't looking. He was holding his hands over his eyes.

"Oh, it's breathtaking!" Jessie exclaimed as she scanned the countryside and the people who looked like midgets so far below her. "Absolutely breathtaking! I can see for miles!"

Ki's fingers split apart and he peered down. He groaned and quickly covered his eyes again.

"I never knew you were afraid of heights," Jessie said, as she continued to survey the world below her in all its wonder.

"Not afraid. Terrified."

"My, but don't this look like we're sitting up on top of the world, though?" cried the third passenger in the gondola, the young man who had come aboard after Jessie and Ki.

"It most certainly does," Jessie agreed, a smile brightening her face at the boy's expression of delight that was blended with amazement.

"I reckon I've been born to be nothing much more than a clodhopper," the boy continued. "But being up here— I'm going to memorize every single minute of this. Then, when I'm marching along behind the plow next time, I'll make-believe pretend that I'm not grounded deep in the muck but flying high like some old beady-eyed bird. I swear that's what I'm going to do!"

"It's warmer up here," Jessie observed. "I guess that's because we're so much closer to the sun up here than down there."

She looked down at the people on the fairgrounds at the edge of town, some of whom were waving, their heads tilted back, hands on their hats to hold them in place. She waved back. The wind that the balloon rode sent it swirling to the east and then, shifting, sent it whirling back the way it had come.

Ki peeked through his fingers to assure himself that the thick rope that held the balloon, running from the basket to the ground, was still in the hands of Professor Bixby's assistant.

It was.

He widened the gap between his fingers and looked up. Clouds drifted above the balloon. He was surprised to discover that they had no more substance than an early morning mist on spring meadows.

"It's disillusioning," he said.

"What is?" Jessie asked him.

"The clouds. From down on earth they look like cotton. But not up here. That's the trouble with firsthand knowledge. It turns the bright light of fact on dreams and the dreams die from the glare."

"Hoo-*eee*!" the young man in the gondola cried, taking off his straw hat and slapping his thigh with it. "Ain't this here trip something worth writing home about, though?"

Jessie had to agree. The sight of the verdant earth below— so far below—was exhilarating. To see things from this perspective—the small houses, the small farms, the still-smaller people—it made her feel not only awed but also humbled.

"What's that?" a startled Ki exclaimed as the gondola lurched suddenly. "Are we going to crash?"

"Naw," answered the young man, putting his hat back on. "They're tugging on the rope to bring us down."

Ki let out a sigh of relief.

Jessie let out a sigh of disappointment.

As the balloon was drawn down to the earth, the clouds seemed to shoot up into the sky above them, where they resumed their thick fleecy forms. The sun seemed to cool. The horizon slipped out of sight.

Professor Bixby's assistant tethered the balloon in place a few minutes later, and the professor himself helped Jessie climb down to the ground.

"What was it like?" a woman hesitantly asked the three passengers.

"Like we was eagles, ma'am," answered the young man with a gleam in his eyes. "Like we was two kings and a queen of the world for the little while we got to spend up there."

"It was wonderful," Jessie answered the woman.

"That's the word, ma'am," the young man said, eagerly nodding his head. "Full of wonder is what it was like up there."

The woman looked at the tall man with the gaunt face standing next to her, hope in her eyes.

He looked back at her, then up at the balloon. "Two dollars, that's dear, Matilda," he said solemnly. "We could buy enough seed corn to plant thirty acres for two dollars."

"Two dollars isn't dear, Lem," Matilda said, her voice firm. "Not when it'll buy us the sky for a few minutes out of our lives."

Lem looked at her, saw the hope swimming in her eyes, and said, "I'll help you climb into that contraption, Matilda. Watch your step."

Jessie stood watching as Lem did, Ki by her side, the young man gone off into the crowd. "That woman has good sense," she said to herself. "The sky's worth twice two dollars any day of the week."

"Let's get out of here," Ki suggested, "before you take a notion to try to get me back into that thing again."

"As a matter of fact—"

"Jessie, no!" Ki took her by the hand and led her past the tent where the pie-and-produce judging was taking place, and over to a large tent set on the western edge of the fairgrounds.

"This is what I've been wanting to see." He pointed to the billboard in front of the tent which announced:

SPECIAL ATTRACTION!

COME ONE! COME ALL!

The Famous Bull-Killing Bear

BEHEMOTH
Will Fight a Bull Today at 2 P.M.

The Bear will be chained with a twenty-foot chain in the middle of the arena. The Bull will be perfectly wild, young, and of the Spanish breed and the best to be found in the country. The Bull's horns will be left at their natural length and not sawed off to prevent accidents.

"It's almost two o'clock now," Ki declared. "Let's go in."

Jessie demurred, saying, "This is not for me. It's not my cup of tea at all. I once watched a bullfight in Mexico City and was sick for an entire day afterward."

"You forced me into that flying machine awhile ago and now you won't do what I want to do," Ki complained as he approached the ticket booth, where tickets were selling fast to a crowd of men who were eagerly laying their money down.

"I'll see you later, Ki."

"Where are you going?"

"I'm just going to wander about and see the sights. We can rendezvous over by the lemonade stand when this gruesome spectacle is over." Jessie, with a wave, turned and disappeared in the crowd.

Ki shrugged, mildly disappointed at her refusal to attend the bull and bear fight with him, and then bought his ticket. He went inside the tent to find that an arena measuring a good forty square feet had been constructed inside it. A five-barred wooden fence separated it from the surrounding tiers of bleacher seats.

He handed his ticket to the man collecting them and climbed up into the bleachers, where he finally found an empty seat near the top of the tier. He sat down, squeezed in between a barn-shouldered man on his left and a bespectacled man on his right who wore a derby hat and spats. Down below, between the fence and the sloping tiers of seats, two fiddlers strolled, playing merry tunes on their instruments and, in the case of one of them, doing a sure-footed little dance from time to time.

While waiting for the contest to begin, Ki scanned the crowd. It contained mostly men—cowboys, well-dressed townsmen who might have been tinhorn gamblers, farmers, a few Indians, and a pair of Mexican women who puffed furiously on the *cigarillos* they held in their jeweled fingers. Ki watched the women. They looked excited as they fidgeted in their seats and talked animatedly to one another.

In the center of the arena beyond the protective fence the

bear, Behemoth, tethered by his chain, prepared to do battle by using his paws to scoop out a large hole several inches deep in the dirt floor of the arena. The animal's growling formed an ominous counterpart to the conversations of the spectators.

A collective roar went up from the throats of the spectators as a wooden door swung open on one side of the arena and the bull came racing into the arena. It started to circle, its head tossing, and then came to a skidding halt as it spotted the bear, which was hunkered down in the shallow pit it had dug for itself and watching it with its tiny black eyes.

The bull stood its ground for a moment amid the dust its sudden halt had raised. Saliva slid from its lips and fell to the ground.

"Get him, Behemoth!" a man below Ki yelled.

"Make mincemeat out of him, bull!" someone else pleaded at the top of his husky voice.

The nameless bull bellowed.

Behemoth flattened itself against the ground.

As the bull charged the bear, many in the crowd sprang to their feet, cheering the animal on, Ki conspicuously not among them. He was silently rooting for the bear in what he considered an uneven battle. The chain, he felt, placed the bear at a decided disadvantage from the very start, making it the underdog in the essentially unfair contest.

Horns lowered, the bull attacked the bear, hitting it heavily in the side and drawing blood, but apparently doing no serious damage because the bear, in response to the attack, sat up and seized the bull's nose in its iron jaws.

The bull bellowed in pain, the sound emerging as a series of rattling snorts because of the bear's fierce grip on its muzzle.

The bear tightened its grip on the bull's nose. The bull shook its head, desperately trying to break free as blood continued to flow from its muzzle. Its efforts finally met with success. It ripped its muzzle free of the bear's jaws and backed away, shaking its head from side to side, blood flying in bright red droplets from its injured nose as it did so.

It pawed the ground as it stood facing the bear, which had

once again flattened itself on the ground as it sought to draw its antagonist down to its level. It growled, a muted thunder.

The sound seemed to stir something in the watching spectators. They let out a collective roar, a kind of growl of their own. The bespectacled man next to Ki clapped a hand on his derby to keep from losing it as the crowd in the bleachers waved their fists in the air and jostled their neighbors. The man's lips worked. Ki was able to make out the word "kill" he mouthed. He stared in some surprise at the seemingly mild-mannered man who was after blood. Was it, he wondered, the bull's or the bear's? He had no time to pursue the speculation because in the arena below the bull once again charged the bear, its head lowered as it tried to hook the bear on its horns.

As if sensing the bull's intention, the bear hunkered down in the shallow pit it had dug for itself and the bull's horns went over its head and body, one of them striking with great force against the wooden pole to which the bear's chain was attached.

The bull pulled its horn free and backed up, its great body swaying, blood still dripping from the muzzle that Behemoth had so successfully savaged.

The man on Ki's left cursed. "This ain't no kind of contest a-tall," he complained. "Look at those two down there doing their fancy little dance. One of 'em should've been deader'n a doornail by now."

The blood lust in the spectators was rising, Ki thought. He hoped it would be the bear that satisfied it by killing the bull, despite the fact that it was chained in place, making it a relatively easy target for its bovine attacker.

The bull lowered its head and pawed the ground, sending up puffs of dust. Its eyes were fastened on the bear, which now sat with forepaws raised in its shallow pit. Waiting. Watching.

When the bull finally charged, the bear dropped down onto its belly, rolled over, reached up with all four paws, and clawed at the unprotected belly of the bull.

Ki let out a loud cheer as the bear drew blood and then with another slashing movement of its paws, tore a length of gray-white intestine out of the bull's belly. But the bull, undeterred by its serious wound, tried desperately to gore the bear, still lying on its side on the ground beneath its enemy.

The bull's horns dug harmlessly into the ground. At one point, the body of the bear was pinned between the long horns. But, then, as the bull raised its head to try again to gore its opponent, Behemoth slid out of the way and slashed downward with one of its forepaws. The blow caught the bull on the head and, as the paw was withdrawn, one of the bull's eyes was ripped out of its socket.

The bull made a shrill sound that could only be called a scream. The bear seemed to smile as it slashed again and then again, ripping the bull's hide in several strategic places. The bull turned and fled. Then it stopped. Turned back. It stood there, a badly wounded warrior, and glared at the bear. It kicked up some dust, but only halfheartedly. Its bloody nostrils flared.

The bear watched the bull's movements, seemingly bracing itself for another attack. When it came, the bear was ready for it—but to no avail. Through a series of badly timed moves on the part of the bear combined with a lucky lunge on the part of the bull, the bear was caught on the bull's right horn, lifted bodily up into the air, and then thrown down to the ground.

Almost at once, the bear struggled to its feet. It raised a clawed paw and slashed at the bull, but missed its target.

As if excited by its successful attack, the bull lunged again. This time its left horn caught the bear in the chest. Squealing, the impaled bear was raised high above the bull's head and then thrown, like a toy no longer wanted by an aggressive child, down to the ground. The animal lay there, its chest ripped open, blood pouring from the ugly red cavity.

As the bull stood motionless and breathing heavily, more of its intestines slipped from the wound in its belly to lie in a glistening pile beneath its body. It swung its head, the movement a weak one.

The bear didn't stir. Its wounded chest heaved mightily and then moved no more. Its eyes glazed as blood no longer spurted from its body because its heart had stopped pumping it.

The bull went down on the knees of its front legs. Its head bent forward until its horns touched the ground only inches away from where the dead bear lay.

The crowd roared, and then gradually quieted as a man with a gun entered the arena and moved cautiously to where the bull now lay on one side, eyelids twitching convulsively. When the man was close enough, he took aim with the gun in his hand and put a bullet in the bull's brain.

The crowd began to leave the arena, some of the spectators collecting on bets they had made, others paying off. Ki made his way among the people filling the bleachers, and when he reached the ground level he headed for the entrance to the tent. Almost as soon as he emerged from the tent, the sight of brightly painted canvas panels met his eyes. They almost stopped him in his tracks.

He went toward them, mesmerized by the painted pictures of beautiful women—blondes, brunettes, redheads—attired in exotic and erotic costumes of colorful diaphanous material as they danced to the tune of a painted flute player seated cross-legged behind them.

"Step right up, and for the price of just ten cents, one thin dime, enter a world of enticing delights and wonderful sights."

The barker in front of the tent that sported the painted panels of the women dancing wore a straw boater and carried a cane, which he waved about in an effort to attract an audience from among the men emerging from the tent where the bull and bear fight had just ended. Many of them eagerly headed in his direction, Ki among them.

"Come closer, gents," the barker said to them as they huddled in front of his stand. "Let me tell you a little about what awaits you on the inside." He turned and gestured toward the tent's entrance with his cane. "In there, gents," he continued, glancing over his shoulder at his wide-eyed audience, "lies a land of magic and mystery, not to mention marvels. In there is a land where women live who know how to stir the blood of a man and make him wild with desire."

The barker turned toward his audience and leaned over his stand. "One thin dime, gents. That's all it takes to buy a ticket to see the lovely ladies waiting inside. They will dance for you. They will delight you or you get your money, every single cent of it, back, I promise you. The ladies inside this tent, gents, are waiting for you right now in all their loveliness and desire. See them dance. See the star of our show, Fatima, wiggle her way across our stage like a reptile as she shakes and she shimmies. . . ."

There was more, but Ki paid no attention to it as he shouldered his way through the crowd to buy a ticket.

Once inside, he waited impatiently with the other members of the audience for the promised performance to begin. It did, about ten minutes later, with the drawing aside of a purple curtain to reveal a painted backdrop of minarets and mosques. Music began. A hidden flute played. An invisible drum beat a soft tattoo.

A gasp went up from the spectators as a woman wearing gauzy pantaloons, two small patches of ruby cloth over her breasts, and nothing else but a veil over the lower half of her face, undulated out onto the stage.

Ki stared in a kind of amazed rapture at her as she bent, twisted, turned, bent again, her arms waving, her eyes sparkling.

She was followed by a pair of identically dressed women who did a dance that simulated the services the slave girls they portrayed delivered to a muscular, bare-chested man who wore a turban and played perfectly the part of a jaded sultan.

At last, Fatima, the star of the show, appeared. She glided into sight and began to dance, her movements the most erotic Ki had ever seen outside of a bedroom. He watched her, fascinated, as she discarded items of her clothing while still managing to preserve what some might call her modesty.

He felt himself stiffening as she dipped and flowed about the stage, finally discarding her azure veil to reveal sloe eyes and full lips painted red. He wanted her. So, he knew, did every other man in the audience. They leaned forward, their jaws agape, as they watched her, desire alight in their hungry eyes.

Fatima winked and Ki was sure it had been at him, but he was just as sure that every other man in the audience undoubtedly believed that she had winked at *him*.

Then, like a dream fading, the performance was over— far too soon to suit Ki. He rose reluctantly and left the tent with the other men. Outside he lingered, looking up at the painted panel that depicted Fatima, and suppressed a sigh before turning and heading for the lemonade stand where he had agreed to rendezvous with Jessie.

"Psst!"

The sibilant sound caused Ki to turn to find the barker for the show he had just seen standing a short distance away and beckoning to him.

"Me?" he asked, and when the barker nodded, he went over to the man.

"I saw you watching the girls in the show," the barker declared. "You look like a gentleman of discretion, and so I thought I would have a word with you in private."

Ki waited.

"The girls are, shall we say, accessible under certain circumstances."

"Accessible?" Ki was sure he knew what the barker meant, though possibly, he admitted to himself, he was merely engaging in wishful thinking.

"They're friendly," the barker amplified, "and willing to make themselves available to men of proper means."

"How much," Ki asked bluntly, "for Fatima?"

"Aha!" the barker cried, smirking. "You know how to pick the cream of the crop, all right. Fatima's favors don't come cheap. Perhaps you'd be interested in one of the other girls?"

"What does Fatima charge for the pleasure of her company?" Ki persisted.

"Two dollars for fifteen minutes."

"Fifteen minutes!" Ki exclaimed. "I can't even get my trousers unbuttoned in fifteen minutes."

The barker shrugged. "That's the going rate, and cheap

enough it is considering what you get for it, I can assure you. Fatima—the other girls as well—has never had a dissatisfied customer. But you have to understand, my dear sir, that their time is money. They are professionals, as you know, who must entertain for a living. Between shows, they occasionally entertain—differently. Are you interested?"

Ki was most definitely interested. "Look," he said, glancing down the midway, "I have to meet a friend of mine. But then I'll be right back to take you up on your offer. Will you be here?"

The barker shook his head. "I'll be behind the tent where the girls perform. But don't dawdle, sir. If you do, you may miss out on the chance of a lifetime. The girls have another performance scheduled in less than an hour. A word to the wise is, I trust in your case, sir, sufficient."

"I'll be seeing you shortly."

As the barker faded into the crowd, Ki made his way to the lemonade stand, where he found Jessie waiting for him. By her side was a man he recognized—Mel Bronson, a rancher who had a far-flung spread not far from Jessie's own cattle ranch.

"I thought you'd disappeared," Jessie declared when he joined them. "How was the show?"

Ki began to blush, and then realized that Jessie was referring to the bull and bear fight, not the dancing girls he had just watched. "Fine," he said, recovering his composure. "Fine and dandy. Glad to see you again, Mr. Bronson."

"It's good to see you again, Ki," Bronson said as the two men shook hands. "Even though we're neighbors, it seems we seldom see one another. I blame business. It keeps us all hopping, doesn't it, Jessie?"

"You're right on that score, Mel. It most certainly does."

Turning to Ki again, Bronson said, "Jessie and I were just talking about the way hardcases and assorted gunslicks seem to be taking over this part of Texas. I refer to the recent highway robberies and stagecoach holdups, not to mention the spate of killings that have plagued the area of late."

"Or the rustling," Jessie added. "Did you hear, Mel, that Matthew Dolan lost nearly a hundred head last week when

14

rustlers stampeded his stock in the middle of the night?"

"I heard," Bronson replied glumly. "I don't know what this world is coming to, I really don't. But I'll tell you one thing. I'm not going to put up with it much longer."

"What are you going to do?" Jessie inquired.

"I'm not sure. Contact my Congressman maybe. Although the politicians in Washington, and the state capital as well, are more interested in lining their own pockets than protecting the interests of their constituents. But somebody has to do something because the lawless are taking over everywhere, it seems. None of us is safe in our own beds anymore."

Jessie turned to Ki and asked, "Are you ready to head home?"

Ki hesitated. "Well, actually I thought I'd stay around the fairgrounds awhile. The place fascinates me and I want to make sure I don't miss a thing."

"Well, I think I'll head home. I'll pick up my horse at the livery in town and see you later, Ki."

"I'll go with you, Jessie," Bronson volunteered. "My surrey's at the livery. We can tie your horse to it and I'll drive you home."

"But, Mel, it's out of your way."

"So it is, so it is. But that is an asset, my dear. It will give me more time to spend with you, which is always a distinct pleasure."

"Go ahead, Jessie," Ki urged. "Take the man up on his offer before he changes his mind."

Jessie smiled and took the arm Bronson offered her. Ki watched them walk down the midway, and then he turned and hurried back to the rear of the tent that housed the dancing girls. There he found the barker and several other men who were eagerly handing over money to the barker. Once having done so, they ducked under the flap of the tent's rear entrance.

"I thought this was going to be a private affair," Ki told the barker when the last of the men had disappeared inside the tent.

"It is, sir, I assure you. In your case—Fatima is waiting

for you. I did not make an appointment for her with any of the other gentlemen."

As the barker held out his hand, Ki rummaged about in the pockets of his trousers and came up with two dollars, which he handed over.

"Inside and to the right, sir. You'll see a canvas dressing room there, and inside it you'll find every lonely man's dream of joy and delight—the lovely, the sultry, the seductive Fatima!"

Ki left the barker and went inside the tent, which he found to be cluttered with boxes and crates of all kinds and sizes. Ahead of him was the rear of the stage, which was bordered by racks of costumes and piles of props. From behind walls of canvas haphazardly strung on ropes he could hear muted female giggles and occasional deep male grunts, both of which bore eloquent testimony to what was taking place behind the flimsy walls.

Where—there!

Fatima's dressing room was readily recognizable by its paper star, which had been cut from a mail-order catalog and pinned to the canvas wall above painted letters: FATIMA. What to do? You couldn't knock on canvas walls. Ki approached the enclosure, and as he did so a sheer gauze veil was tossed over its top to hang there like a delicate beacon urging him on.

"Miss?" he said out loud. "Miss Fatima?"

At once, the canvas was drawn aside and Ki found himself facing the object of his rampant desire. She was smiling and holding out her hand to him. He reached out and took it and let her lead him inside, which turned out to be cluttered with trunks and racks of costumes.

"I've been waiting for you," Fatima said, showing Ki to a chair in the midst of the clutter. "I recognized you at once."

"You did? How?"

"I saw you in the audience. Later, Johnny, the barker, told me he had someone for me who was far more exotic than I am. What are you, a Jap or a Chinaman?"

"You hit it right the first time out. I'm Japanese. Well, half-Japanese anyway. And half-Caucasian."

"I'm Scotch-Irish with a dash of Cherokee Indian thrown in for good measure. I'll tell you a secret. My name's not really Fatima. That's my professional name. My real name's Ida Groat. Isn't that a scream? I graduated from Ida Groat to Fatima without hardly any trouble at all. But you didn't come here to talk, did you?"

Ki shook his head.

"I was sure you didn't." A coquettish smile from Ida Groat, alias Fatima. Then a hot touch of her hand on Ki's cool cheek. Followed by a flickering of her ten slender fingers as they busied themselves unbuttoning his trousers. "We've been wasting time—*I've* been. Did Johnny tell you you've only got fifteen minutes?"

"What does Johnny do, stand outside with a stop-watch?"

"Not exactly. But he does keep track of the time, so let's be about our business. Oh, my, yours is longer when it's still soft than most men's are when they're hard."

Ki wasn't sure if he had just been complimented or insulted. Fatima's tone, though marveling, was neutral.

"What kind of sex do half-Japanese men such as yourself like?" Fatima asked with no trace of coyness.

Ki told her, and she promptly went to a cot in a corner of the canvas enclosure and sat down upon it. He watched her strip away the few clothes she was wearing and then, as she lay down on her back on the cot, he hurriedly undressed, mindful of the minutes passing. He had visions of the barker bursting in on them and demanding that he get out without giving him time to dress, let alone finish his business with the lady on the bed whose sloe-eyed gaze was roaming up and down his body.

He went to her, knelt on the bed, and then almost pounced on her. She welcomed him with open arms and a skillful hand that gripped his stone-stiff shaft and guided it into her. As he began to buck, she shifted position beneath him until she had fitted herself to him perfectly and arousingly. She soon matched his rhythm, moaning softly as she did so, her pelvis doing a swift sensuous dance as it rose to meet his eager thrusts.

17

He felt himself soaring into a kind of ecstasy as their coupling continued. All that he was, all that he felt, seemed to suddenly become centered in his loins as his body slapped sweatily against the woman whose soft arms had enfolded him and whose lean and limber legs were wrapped tightly around his thighs. He felt oddly light-headed. His skin tingled. His toes tightened and began to curl.

"Do it," she whispered, and tightened her grip on him. "Uh, uh, *uh!*"

Ki climaxed only seconds after she did. He exploded within his lusty partner, and she cried out as he did so and tossed her head from side to side.

Ki's breath gusted in and out of his nose and open mouth. His heart pounded, but his body began to relax. He stopped bucking and lay upon the lady sharing the cot with him, his lips nuzzling her earlobe, his fingers running lightly up and down her sides, causing her to tremble.

"You finished well within the time limit," she said, and pushed him off her.

The feelings of satisfaction, relief, and roiling ecstasy that engulfed him promptly vanished. The ordinary world returned and he was once again inside the tawdry dressing room with Fatima-Ida, and he knew, somewhat sadly, that nothing lasted. But he also knew that some things—like lust—though not lasting, were a thrilling source of satisfaction while they did remain with a man.

He got up and began to dress as Fatima put on what he assumed was the spangled costume she would wear in her next performance—her next *public* performance.

"I suppose we won't meet again," she remarked offhandedly. "But I want you to know it was real nice. If you're ever at another county fair somewhere, you be sure to look to see if I'm working it, will you?"

"You bet," Ki promised, and then left the tent, taking with him a blazingly bright image of Ida Groat—no, Fatima—which brightened his day.

★

Chapter 2

Ki, riding home from the county fair aboard his blood bay, which he had picked up at the livery in town, was passing Mel Bronson's spread when he heard a series of loud whoops from somewhere up ahead of him. He rode on, the horse beneath him moving stolidly, and as he rounded a bend he saw the source of the whoops.

Three cowboys were riding and whooping loudly as they rode hell-for-leather across the open range for no reason that Ki at first could see. But then, as the cowboys, whose backs, were to him, swerved and headed back toward him, he saw the pair of coyotes that the men had been pursuing.

A few head of cattle, seeing themselves in the path of the oncoming cowboys, lumbered lazily out of the way and then lowered their heads to graze again. The cowboys went galloping past them and on toward Ki, who quickly removed the lariat that hung from his saddlehorn, shook it out, and began to whirl a wide loop above his head.

As the pair of coyotes cut to the right to avoid him, he slammed spurs into his bay's flanks and went after them. Behind him the cowboys turned and went after him, still whooping at the tops of their voices, their own lariats in the air as they rode.

"Catch the critters, Ki!" yelled one of the three, a man named Henry Longus whom Ki had met at a barn dance a month earlier. "Don't let the chicken-thieving sonsabitches get away!"

Ki set his loop flying through the air ahead of him. It came down and around the neck of the coyote that was racing along in front of its companion. He jerked it tight and the coyote was yanked backward and then up into the air. As Ki reeled in his rope, the coyote fell back to the ground and bounced along it. Two of the cowboys rode on past him, but Longus drew rein when Ki did and slapped him on the back. "Congratulations, my friend! You done did it. You got the bastard."

Ki dismounted. Keeping a tight grip on his rope, he threw its free end over the limb of a cottonwood growing on the bank of a narrow stream.

"String him up!" Longus cried.

Ki did. Hauling on one end of the rope, he soon had the coyote he had lassoed around the neck hanging in the middle of the air.

The animal's paws worked furiously but helplessly as if it were scrabbling on some solid surface in an attempt to gain purchase. Its eyes were wide—bulging—their whites plainly visible. Its tail worked, seeming to pump the air, as its tongue slid out of its gaping jaws.

Longus reached out and gave Ki's taut rope a sturdy jerk and then another one. Each pull on the rope jerked the coyote up into the air, and then it fell heavily back to hang suspended.

Seconds later, its struggles ended. Its body seemed to extend itself unnaturally and then fold in upon itself, its hind legs rising and then dropping downward again. It released a flood of urine, and then its bowels released their malodorous contents.

"Sure does stink, don't it?" Longus commented, holding his nose. "Let's get out of here. See if the boys caught the other one yet."

Ki freed his rope, tossed the carcass of the coyote aside, and climbed back into the saddle. He coiled his rope as he rode out behind Longus in the direction taken by the other two cowboys.

"Those infernal critters have been playing havoc with Mr. Bronson's chickens," Longus announced as they rode. "Damn near ever' night they get into the chicken coop and oh, my, but don't the feathers fly then!"

"We've had the same problem on the Starbuck ranch," Ki remarked. "We lost half a dozen Rhode Island Reds to coyotes. And all of them, every one, were hens. Seems the coyotes don't have a taste for rooster, just female flesh."

"Old Virge Prentiss lost two lambs to them a while back," Longus volunteered. "Coyotes'll prey on anything weak and helpless."

"Well, there's one less of them on the range as of now."

"Look! Bob and Custis have the other one on the run."

Ki looked in the direction they were traveling and saw the two cowboys Longus had named riding toward them, the coyote they had been chasing covering the ground in a blur of fur as it raced toward Ki and Longus.

Ki formed a loop and let it fly, but he missed his target.

Longus, when he threw his lariat, didn't miss. His rope encircled the coyote's neck, and then the animal was flying through the air in a wide circle as a happily whooping Longus swung his lariat over his head.

Longus, still swinging his lariat, rode toward a sycamore growing in the distance. As he neared it, he took aim and slammed the still-living coyote against the tree's thick trunk, smashing its skull and most of the other bones in the animal's body.

"That's the end of him," Longus gloated, untying the animal's lifeless body and tossing it aside.

"How you been?" asked Custis as he pulled up beside Ki, who was rolling up his rope.

"Fine, Custis, just fine. Yourself?"

"Me and Bob here have been having some fun twirling our lariats," Custis replied.

"Instead of our mustaches," Bob interjected with a grin.

"But it was you who got one of the critters," Custis observed. "So you get to collect the bounty on its pelt."

"How much they paying these days per pelt?" Ki inquired as he rehung his lariat on his saddlehorn.

"Six, up from five last month," Custis replied.

"Tell you what," Ki said. "You three turn in those two pelts and split the twelve dollars. All I ask is you have a drink in my name when you get around to spending your bonanza."

"Generous to a fault as always, that's you," Longus commented. "But why don't you come along with us while we drive those strays we rounded up over there back onto Mr. Bronson's range, and then we can all three of us go into town, sell the pelts, and paint our noses till the money runs out."

"I appreciate the offer and have to say it's a truly tempting one," Ki said, "but I've got to get back to the ranch. See you boys another time."

Ki swung into the saddle and moved his horse out with a wave to the three cowboys he was leaving behind. He headed west, and was about to round a bend when he heard the sound of a shot—from a carbine judging by the pinging it made. He drew rein and turned his horse.

Four men were riding down on Longus, Custis, and Bob. All of them were armed and there was no mistaking their intent. They were after the cows the three cowboys had rounded up before Ki came upon them.

Ki patted his vest pocket to reassure himself that his *shuriken*, his five-pointed and -bladed throwing stars, were where he usually kept them. Then he put heels to his horse and rode back the way he had come. He moved in among some post oaks growing below a ridge, and walked his horse through them until he reached the outer edge of the grove. There he sat his saddle watching what was taking place a few hundred yards away from his position, waiting for a chance to make a move.

"Throw down your guns, you three!" he heard the man who was apparently the leader of the rustlers order.

Longus and his two companions did as they had been told.

One of the four rustlers dismounted and retrieved the dropped guns.

"Now you boys be sensible and nothing's going to happen to you," said the man who had spoken earlier. "But if you try anything foolish, I'll let light through you. You all got that?"

None of the three men to whom the man had spoken answered him. They merely continued standing where they were, their hands in the air.

Ki dismounted and, leaving his horse ground-hitched, left the cover of the woods. Keeping low, he ran, his body bent over, to where the cows were contentedly grazing, unmindful of the potential danger surrounding them. Ducking down behind the cattle, he forced his way in among them, heading through them toward the spot where the rustlers were standing with their backs to him.

The cows lowed as he shouldered his way through their midst. One of them bellowed, causing one of the gunmen to glance over his shoulder.

But Ki had dropped to one knee and was not visible to the curious man who had turned in his direction.

Moments later, Ki resumed his potentially perilous journey, stepping nimbly to avoid being stepped upon, until he was within reaching distance of the man who had dismounted and was holding the guns taken from the three cowboys employed by Mel Bronson.

"You want us to move these cows out now, Pete?" one of the men asked.

"Now's as good a time as any," the leader of the quartet replied. "Sam, you keep your gun on those three until we've put some distance between us and them. Then you can catch up with us."

As one of the rustlers was about to turn his horse, Ki made his move. He threw himself forward, both hands reaching. He got a solid grip on the shoulders of the man holding the small confiscated arsenal and pulled him backward. As the man lost his balance and fell to the ground, Ki stooped, swooped up two of the guns the man had been holding, and tossed them to Longus and Bob.

As the cowboys caught the weapons, Ki threw one of his *shuriken*. It hit one of the rustlers in the shoulder, causing him to drop his gun.

At the same instant, Longus fired the gun Ki had tossed to him. But his shot missed the man named Pete, who promptly returned the fire, hitting Longus in the upper left arm.

The man Ki had downed scrambled to his feet and lunged. But Ki was ready for him with a raised leg and a flying foot that slammed into the man's lower jaw, snapping his head backward and sending him teetering backward, his arms flailing wildly as he fought to stay on his feet—and failed.

As the man went down a second time, Ki ran to him, pulled him up, and using him as a shield, called out, "If any of you boys makes another move your friend here's dead. I'll throttle him."

"He's bluffing," one of the rustlers muttered to no one in particular, and raised the gun in his hand.

Ki wrapped his right forearm around his captive's throat and squeezed.

"Aaagghh!"

The strangled sound his prisoner made was enough to make the man named Pete hold up his free hand to signal to his men to hold their fire.

"Let Billy go," Pete said. "We'll take him and ride out of here."

"Get some rope," Ki called out to Longus, Bob, and Custis "Tie these men up. We'll take them back to town and let the marshall decide what's to be done with them."

As the three cowboys went to their horses to get their ropes, Ki continued holding tightly to his prisoner as the man clawed at his forearm in a vain effort to free himself.

"Pete," one of the rustlers said. When he had the man's attention, he continued. "I'm not going back to jail. I'd rather be dead than spend another hour in jail. I've spent half of my young life there and I'll be damned if I'm going back again!"

"Take it easy, Pritchard," Pete cautioned. "This party's not over yet. Matter of fact, it's still going strong."

Ki caught the sly glance that Pete had given the man Ki was close to throttling, but before he could interpret its meaning his captive kicked backward with one foot.

The man's heavy boot slammed into Ki's left shin, sending pain screaming up his leg and into his brain. Responding reflexively to it, he lost his grip on his captive. The man spun around and swung a fist, which caught Ki on the side of the head, sending sparkling stars careening across his line of sight.

Ki heard the sound of several shots, but he couldn't see who had fired at whom because he was doubled over as a result of the kick and the roundhouse right he had just taken. He tried to escape from the knee he suddenly saw coming up fast toward him, but he reacted an instant too late. The knee slammed into his face with the sickening sound of bone smashing against bone. Then the lights Ki had been seeing vanished, and he found himself lost in a world that had suddenly turned black.

As consciousness returned to him like a slow tide washing up on a battered shore, Ki felt pressure on his neck. He tried to move it as the blackness began to give way to a thick grayness, and found he could not.

His eyes eased open as the pressure intensified and he heard the sound of voices:

"—the whole bunch'll have reason to remember Pete Damson after today."

"Two of those cowboys are past remembering anything, Pete."

Ki became aware that a knee was pressing down hard on the back of his neck and someone—he finally managed to catch a glimpse of the man from his prone position on the ground, it was the one named Pritchard—was tying his hands as he knelt on Ki's neck.

Ki struggled to free himself, but quickly found he was unable to do so.

Then there was a figure looming over him, one that blotted

out the orange light of the lowering sun. Ki blinked and managed to make out the stubbled face of Pete Damson, who was staring down at him.

"It's time you were taught a lesson," Damson muttered.

At the same time, Pritchard removed his knee from Ki's neck and stood up.

Ki managed to get to a sitting position, but he had no sooner done so than Damson kicked out at him, catching him in the chest with one booted foot and sending him toppling back down to the ground.

But Ki had managed to catch a glimpse of his surroundings and had seen the two bodies lying some distance away, both of them twisted into unnatural shapes, both of them bloodstained. The bodies, he had been able to make out, were of the cowboys named Bob and Custis. Near them stood Longus, holding his wounded left arm, while Damson's man whom Ki had wounded with his *shuriken* held his gun on him.

Ki scrambled to his feet, his hands bound in front of him, and was about to swing them at Damson when the leader of the rustlers swiftly stepped aside to avoid the blow as he yelled, *"Pritchard!"*

Ki was jerked off his feet by Pritchard, who, aboard a gray gelding, had jerked the other end of the rope he held in his hand. He laughed as Ki went down and then, dallying the rope around his saddlehorn, he moved his mount out and Ki was dragged along the ground.

He tried to get to his feet, but there was no way he could do so as Pritchard spurred his gray and the animal began to trot. Ki gripped the rope in his fingers and pulled in what he knew was a hopeless effort to halt Pritchard's horse. He heard laughter coming from behind him, and the sound of it enraged him. Pete Damson and the others were enjoying themselves at his expense.

He gritted his teeth as dust rose up around him and his body bounded helplessly along the rough ground that was grassy only in spots. His shoulders ached and his arms seemed about to snap out of their sockets. He tried to hold his head as high off the ground as possible in order not to

26

suffer injury to his eyes, but it was an almost impossible task to do so. He settled for lowering his head so that his lower jaw touched his chest. That way, he hoped, he might have less chance of a fatal injury to his head.

He opened his mouth to suck in air and sucked in a great quantity of dust along with it, which made him gag. His eyes began to stream tears as a result of the dust irritating them.

His shirt was soon in tatters, and his vest ripped and tore away from his body as Pritchard rode in a circle, slapping his horse with his reins, and his companions continued laughing, a sound like wolves baying.

The world whirled around Ki as he bounced along the ground, which badly abraded his skin. He rolled helplessly from side to side. He choked off a scream as a patch of gravel tore at his body, drawing blood from both his chest and back.

He was suddenly jerked sharply to the right. He squinted through the sun-lanced clouds of dust and saw that Pritchard had changed course. Ki almost cried out when he saw the expanse of boulders spread out directly ahead of him over which Pritchard's gray was stumbling. He wanted to close his eyes to block out the sight of them, but found he could not. As they loomed closer and closer to him, he tried to roll out of their way, but his efforts came to naught because of the speed with which Pritchard's horse was traveling, which kept Ki's arms stretched straight out in front of him, preventing any such ploy.

Then the first of the boulders slammed into his left shoulder with savage force. Another one seemed to come rolling rapidly toward him. This one struck the top of his head and gave him an instantaneous gift of mercy that took the form of sudden unconsciousness.

"Ki."

The sound of his name being spoken roused Ki. He seemed to be swimming through the inky blackness that enveloped him as he tried to return to consciousness.

"Ki?"

27

The blackness began to dissipate. Its place was taken by pain. Pain everywhere in Ki's body that raked and rasped, clawed and gouged at him. His eyes opened.

The sun, he saw, was down. Purple shadows, some of them slowly fading to black, covered the ground, shed by trees and buttes and ridges. The evening star, a tiny silver eye in a reddish sky, winked at him. Ki closed his eyes again and drew a shallow breath, trying to will away the pain that would not be banished.

"I untied your hands," Longus said as he hunkered down beside Ki, who was lying on his back on the ground. "I waited for you to come to. Do you think maybe you can get on your horse? I'll take you to Mr. Bronson's. I gotta go tell him what happened here."

"Bob and Custis . . ."

"They're dead," Longus said dully. "I'm lucky I'm not. So are you, I reckon. Those rustlers led by that Pete Damson killed Bob and Custis in the gunfight that broke out. Not one of them was so much as scratched, sad to say. Except for the one you wounded with that thing you threw."

"The cattle?"

"Gone."

Ki tried to rise, fell back.

Longus helped him sit up. He sat there on the ground, his arms limp at his sides, his head hanging down.

"It's bad, ain't it, Ki?"

"I feel like I've been dragged by a horse." Ki tried a smile that never materialized.

"You want me to help you over to your horse now?"

"Thanks, but no, not yet. I think if I stand up I'm going to fall right back down again. My legs feel like rubber and my gut feels like it's going to throw out every single thing that's in it. I need a few minutes."

Longus remained where he was, saying nothing.

"You go on back to the Bronson place," Ki told him. "You'll need to bring a wagon out here to get the bodies."

"I'll stay with you till you think you can manage by your own self."

The two men said nothing for a time until Ki, feeling some faint semblance of strength returning to his limbs and a settling in his gut, said, "I'm game to try to get to my horse now if you'll let me lean on your shoulder, Longus."

Longus rose and helped Ki to his feet. He steadied his friend, who stood swaying unsteadily for several minutes, and then, looping one of Ki's arms over his uninjured right shoulder, he helped him over to his bay.

Ki put a foot in a stirrup. Got a grip on his saddle horn. Swung his other leg . . .

Longus caught him before he could fall and helped him lean against his mount as sweat blossomed on his face.

Ki tried once again to swing into the saddle, but the same thing happened. He just couldn't do it.

"They say the third time's the charm," he muttered, tightening his grip on the saddlehorn and making another effort to climb into the saddle. This time he was successful. He sat his saddle, both hands gripping his saddlehorn as wave after wave of dizziness washed over him. He squeezed his eyes shut and the dizziness left him. Opening them again, he took the reins Longus handed him.

"I'd better see that you get home safe," Longus said to him.

"I'm obliged to you, my friend."

With that the two men rode out, heading in the direction of Jessie's ranch.

Jessie gave a shocked cry when she opened the door and saw the bloody pair standing outside.

Longus was supporting Ki, whose body sagged as he gripped the door frame for further support. Longus's arm no longer bled, but it had stained his shirt and jeans while it bled and he looked ashen now. Ki's body and clothes were both covered with crusted blood.

"What happened?" Jessie managed to get out as she opened the door wide and Longus helped Ki inside.

"We had a run-in with some rustlers," Longus answered as he helped Ki sit down on a carved wooden bench just inside the door.

Jessie stared at the cowboy, who she knew worked for Mel Bronson but whose name, at the moment, escaped her. "Rustlers?"

"Out near the Bronson spread," Ki said. "They were led by a man named Pete Damson. They killed two of Mr. Bronson's cowboys and made off with some stock."

Jessie gasped, one hand flying up to cover her mouth.

"They decided to torment Ki on account of how he tried to help me and Bob and Custis when they swooped down on us," Longus explained. "They dragged him behind a horse."

Jessie knelt in front of Ki. "I'll get you upstairs and clean you up. I'll bring hot water, alcohol—"

She broke off in mid-sentence, stood, and shook hands with Longus. "I want to thank you sincerely for helping Ki get home. I'm most grateful to you."

"Glad I could help, Miss Starbuck."

As Longus turned to go, Jessie reached out and stopped him. "I'll do what I can for that wound of yours. Help me get Ki upstairs first, though, will you?"

Together they managed to get Ki into one of the upstairs bedrooms, and then, as he rested on his back on the bed, Jessie left the room. When she returned, she brought with her a basin full of hot water, some clean white muslin, and a bottle of alcohol.

"Take off your shirt," she told Longus. When he had done so, she told him to sit down in the chair next to the bed, and then proceeded to clean his wound and sterilize it with the alcohol. She tried to be as gentle as possible, but she was aware of Longus's wincing and how he turned his head away from the sight of his ragged flesh.

"I'm much obliged to you, Miss Starbuck," he said when she had finished bandaging his arm. "I can't say you have the touch of an angel, but you sure do know how to get the job done good."

Jessie smiled wanly as Longus put his shirt back on.

"I'll be on my way now," he told her.

She turned to Ki, who was lying on the bed with his eyes closed, his arms akimbo. She picked up the basin full of bloody water and carried it out of the room. She was back within minutes with clean water that steamed in the basin and some more clean cloths.

She wasted no time in stripping what was left of Ki's shirt and vest from his body. Then she applied hot compresses to his many wounds. She deliberately reopened them and let the blood flow freely in an effort to avoid infection, a procedure she had learned from an Arapaho Indian friend many years earlier. Then she swabbed the open wounds with liberal doses of alcohol, trying to ignore Ki's occasional cries of pain and the severe trembling of his body. She deftly bandaged his wounds, and then quietly left the room when she saw that her friend had lapsed into a deep sleep.

Downstairs, she stood in the kitchen of the ranch and tightly gripped the edge of the sink. She closed her eyes and lowered her head. Behind her eyelids she could see Ki's savaged body. She saw the blood that had covered it just as it had covered Longus's arm and clothes. She imagined what it must have been like for Ki to have been dragged behind the horse of one of the rustlers who had attacked the men who were working for Mel Bronson. She thought of the two cowboys the rustlers had killed. As fury boiled within her, she vowed vengeance against the men— and all others like them—who had so badly hurt her friend and who had been turning the surrounding area into a killing ground during the past few months.

"It's got to stop—it's got to *be* stopped!" Jessie exclaimed several days later to the men gathered in the great room of her ranch for the meeting she had arranged.

"You're right," one of the men declared vigorously, nodding his head. "We're all fed up with the way gunhawks have practically taken over the country around here."

"The question is, how do we stop what's been going on?" Mel Bronson asked, by no means rhetorically, as he stood smoking a quirly by the front door.

No one answered him.

Jessie broke the silence by asking, "Ki, what do you think?"

31

Her friend was seated in a mohair chair near a window. He wore an open shirt over the bandages that still covered most of his chest, and there were jagged lacerations plainly visible on his forehead, nose, and cheeks that were beginning to heal.

"There's the law," he said softly.

"The law," one of the men spat. "I went to the marshal when two of my horses were stolen right out of my barn—right under my nose, so to speak—and what did he tell me? He told me he'd keep an eye out for whoever might have made off with my horses."

As the man snorted his contempt for the law, one of the others in the room, a blue-eyed man with a white goatee and mustache, said, "Marshal Collins does the best job he can under the circumstances, I'd say. He can't be everywhere at once. He's only got two deputies—"

"And one of them—that Whit Price—is a drunk and everybody knows it." Mel Bronson opened the front door and tossed his quirly outside. Then, closing the door again, he said, "I went to see Marshal Collins the day after Damson and his riders killed two of my men and made off with my stock. He promised he'd do what he could to run Damson to ground, but so far he's not done anything. And I'll tell you this. I can't live my life or run my business on promises."

Silence greeted Bronson's words, which had been spoken with some heat.

Finally, Jessie said, "If the law can't do the job that needs doing—" she looked from one man to the next before continuing "—then it may well be time for us to do the job for ourselves."

"Hear, hear!" Bronson said in response to Jessie's words.

"What exactly are you getting at, Miss Starbuck?" asked one of the men.

"Mr. Barker, I think you know what I'm getting at. I think we should form a Vigilance Committee to protect our interests."

"Miss Starbuck," Barker said, "I'm a cattleman, not a gunman. I'm certainly no vigilante."

"God helps those who help themselves," Bronson declared.

Barker looked doubtful.

"When push comes to shove, as it appears to have done here and now," Bronson continued, "I think we have to do whatever has to be done to take back control of our lives and property from the lawless elements on the loose. None of us, I grant you, are gunmen, but all of us, I submit, are men—and women—" Bronson nodded in Jessie's direction "—of guts and git-go. But if anybody doesn't like the idea of forming a Vigilance Committee, well, let him say so now—speak his piece—and that'll be that. I'm sure we can round up enough good volunteers to put the lid on things so that men like Pete Damson will find out we're not such easy pickings anymore."

There were murmurs of agreement among most of the men. One of them stood up, a man named Charles Proctor, and declared, "I for one go along with what Miss Starbuck has suggested. Let's put it to a vote. How many of us are in favor of establishing a Vigilance Committee to fill the gap the law's left in our lives of late?"

Ki said nothing as the vote was taken, trying to ignore the sense of unease that had settled upon him as the stockmen and farmers in the room moved slowly at first, and then more quickly, toward establishing themselves as vigilantes dedicated to protecting themselves, their property, and each other. They used noble words like "honor" and "self-defense" and "righteousness," but those occasionally hot words did nothing to alleviate the uneasiness he was feeling.

"How many does that make us?" Bronson asked when the vote had been taken and most of the men in the room and Jessie had elected to form a Vigilance Committee.

"Nineteen," Proctor answered him, "which sounds like a goodly number to me."

"It is," Bronson agreed. "It most certainly is indeed. It's a number that will help to insure that nothing like what happened to my three men and Ki at the hands of Damson and his rustlers will ever happen again. Or if it does happen again, the nineteen of us will make sure that the perpetrators do not go unpunished."

"One word of caution, if I may," Jessie interjected. When the eyes of the men in the room turned to her, she continued. "I see us operating as an arm of the law. A force that supports it, not supplants it. I think we should all be clear at the outset on that point. Do you agree with me, gentlemen?"

"By all means," a man seated near Ki said firmly. "It will be as if we're unofficial and unsworn deputies of Marshal Collins."

"Does that mean we won't get paid by the county?" someone else asked plaintively.

Laughter erupted in the room.

One of the men said, "Bill there's always thinking about how to turn everything he does or thinks into cold cash."

"So what's wrong with that, may I ask?" Bill inquired with an expression of mock innocence on his face.

More laughter. Then the meeting began to break up.

Jessie saw her guests to the door and thanked them all for coming.

Mel Bronson was the last to leave. "I think your suggestion to form a Vigilance Committee is a fine one, Jessie. To be frank, if you hadn't proposed such a move I would have. I'd had it in mind to do so, as a matter of fact, ever since my two men were killed and Longus was wounded. It's just too bad that we've got a few lily-livered men in the bunch that was here today who won't throw in with us."

"I can understand their positions, Mel. I don't judge them. After all, they're not gunfighters. They're family men and as such, serving on a Vigilance Committee is more than a little out of their line."

"I would have said it was out of my line less than a week ago had anybody asked me about it. But it's not anymore. In the days to come, I'm hoping to have me a chance to even up the score between me and that Pete Damson. He's not going to kill two and wound one of my men and think that's the end of it. It's like the Bible says. 'An eye for an eye and a tooth for a tooth.' "

★

Chapter 3

"Want some more?" Jessie asked Ki two days later as she stirred the batter she had made and he hungrily devoured the plateful of griddle cakes she had just made for him.

He held up a hand, his mouth full, and shook his head. Then, swallowing, he said, "Not that they're not delicious, but I couldn't get even one more down."

"What's the matter? Have you lost your appetite during your convalescence? You only had six griddle cakes, and I can remember you polishing off eight at least without batting an eye."

"You're forgetting that I also had a big piece of goat cheese and two glasses of milk. As for my convalescence, I think that's finally over and done with."

Jessie poured more batter onto her fire-blackened griddle and watched it sizzle, a spatula at the ready in her hand. "You're feeling fit, are you?"

"I've still got a bit of stiffness here and there. But that's to be expected, I suppose. By and large, though, I'm fine. I thought I'd ride out this morning and check the new barbed-wire fence you ordered installed on the northern perimeter of the ranch."

"You're sure you're up to it?" Jessie asked as she flipped her griddle cakes to brown them on the other side.

"Sure. But I have a confession to make."

Jessie gave him a quizzical glance.

Ki grinned. "I'm not so much intent on checking the fence as I am on getting out of the house on top of a good horse. I've developed a bad case of cabin fever during the past few days."

"Nothing wrong with that. There never is when someone combines business and pleasure."

"You're sure about that, are you? I could give you an example or two that might change your mind," Jessie said.

"An example or two from your own experience?"

"From my own bitter experience, yes." Jessie smiled.

Ki drank the last of the coffee in his cup.

Jessie lifted her griddle cakes with her spatula and put them on the dish she had placed in the oven to warm it. She poured herself a cup of coffee and sat down opposite Ki at the table.

She cut part of the griddle cake into bite-size pieces and proceeded to eat, savoring each mouthful. "You're right if I do say so myself. These are delicious."

"Partly because of the huckleberries you put in the batter. Huckleberries to me, along with ripe red tomatoes, symbolize the wonderful tastes of summer."

"Which reminds me. I have to weed my garden this morning. Jimsonweed's gotten into it, and if I don't get it out it's going to strangle my melon vines."

"I'll do it for you while you're finishing your breakfast," Ki volunteered. "I've got to do something around here to earn my keep."

"I'll join you in a few minutes."

Ki rose and went outside, where he found a hoe leaning against the wall of the house on the side where Jessie's kitchen garden was growing. He picked it up and waved it about to shoo the chickens out of the staked tomatoes, and then began digging up the jimson and other weeds that had invaded the garden. Sweat beaded on his forehead as he worked and ran down his back as a result of the midsummer sun that blazed in the cloudless sky.

He paused to touch a half-ripe tomato that was warm and, he imagined, full of sweet juices. He stamped his foot to shoo one of the braver hens, which had returned to forage in the shade of the pole beans growing tall on a network of sticks and strings. The hen, wings spread, went flapping away, clucking in annoyance.

Ki picked a hornworm off one of Jessie's tomato vines and stamped it underfoot. He shifted each vine slightly to get at the weeds growing beneath them. He was finished weeding the tomatoes, and was well into the patch of melons when Jessie emerged from the house to join him.

"I'll take over now," she said, reaching for the hoe.

Ki straightened and handed it to her, wiping sweat from his face with the back of his other hand as he did so. "It's going to be a scorcher today."

"I read in the paper yesterday that somebody fried an egg in the middle of El Paso's main street the other day."

Ki turned and raised a hand to shield his eyes from the glare of the sun. "Somebody's coming."

Jessie looked in the direction he was gazing, but could see no one. But she was sure that Ki was right. He had an almost uncanny way of knowing when someone was coming that was the result of his keen hearing and some other mysterious ability—or maybe more than just one— which she had never yet been able to identify.

"It's Ed Wright," Ki said a moment later as a rider came into view in the distance. "He's riding hard."

Minutes later, Jessie's ranch foreman pulled up beside them, drawing rein, his horse circling. "Jessie, I got some bad news," he announced.

"What is it, Ed?"

The older man took off his hat and ran his fingers through his hair. "I rode over to Big Meadow early this morning to see how the stock we'd pastured there were doing. When I got there, they were gone. It was as if they had up and

37

vanished into thin air. But I knew they hadn't. I heard about what happened to Mel Bronson's stock—how a bunch of his strays were stolen by rustlers. I reckon that's what happened to our cattle."

"You're sure they're gone, Ed?"

"I've no doubt about it. I rode about a bit over in Big Meadow but, like I told you, they're gone. You can see where they were driven off in a northwesterly direction. Somebody had them on the run, judging by the way the ground's torn up out there. I could make out the tracks of at least three riders."

"Pete Damson," Ki muttered under his breath.

"Do you think that's who stole them?" Jessie asked.

"I think it's highly likely," Ki replied. "Damson's been a busy boy lately. It's easy enough to put two and two together and come up with his name."

"It's my fault," Jessie said. "I should have posted guards to watch over the cattle."

"It's as much my fault as it is yours, Jessie," Wright ruefully admitted. "But I'll tell you, the thought of posting guards never even crossed my mind. We've never lost stock like this before."

"Even if you had posted guards," Ki offered, addressing both Jessie and her foreman, "there's no assurance that the rustling wouldn't have taken place anyway. Look at what happened in the Bronson incident. Two men dead, one wounded, and the cows gone."

"Maybe the fact that we had nobody guarding the cattle is a blessing in disguise," Jessie speculated.

"What do you want me to do about what's happened, Jessie?" Wright asked, clapping his hat back on his head.

"Nothing."

"Nothing? That doesn't sound like you, Jessie, if you'll pardon my saying so. You're not just going to let whoever made off with those cows get away scot-free, are you?"

"No, I definitely am not about to do that," Jessie replied firmly. "I'm going to round up some of the members of our Vigilance Committee—as many as are free to ride with me—and we'll go out after the rustlers and the cows they took."

"I heard about that outfit you and Mr. Bronson and some others have set up," Wright volunteered. "It's high time somebody got enough of their dander up to try to put a stop to all the lawlessness that's swept over this part of Texas lately. I'll be glad to ride with you, Jessie."

She shook her head. "You can do more good here, Ed. Send some men out to round up all our stock. Then drive them to some spot where there's good pasture—I'd suggest Paradise Valley—and keep an around-the-clock guard on them."

"I'll do that. Paradise Valley is as good a spot as any. Better than most, as a matter of fact. It's got good high canyon walls on both sides and narrow entrances to it. We can pretty much control things out there. Of course, we'll have to get some guns so we'll be ready just in case something happens."

"Good idea," Jessie said. "The men who ride for Pete Damson are all heavily armed according to Ki."

"I heard you had a bad run-in with those bast—boys," Wright said. "You okay now, are you, Ki?"

"Almost as good as new, Ed. Ready to ride out and see if I can't even up the score some between Damson and me."

Jessie frowned. "I'm not so sure that's a good idea."

"Why not?" Ki asked.

"After what you've been through . . ."

"That's the point, Jessie. I've *been* through it. I'm fit now and raring to go. Sitting around the ranch for the past few days while I was waiting to mend was almost worse punishment than what I got from Damson and his cattle thieves."

"Thanks, Ed, for riding in to let me know what's happened," Jessie said.

"You're sure you don't want me to side you?"

"No, you've got a more important job to do, as we discussed. There'll be enough of us—more than enough of us, I hope—to teach Damson and his men a lesson or two."

"Call me Professor Ki," Ki said with a faint smile. "I can't wait to start teaching those miscreants a lesson—and I don't mean sums or fractions."

• • •

By noon of that day, Jessie had rounded up Mel Bronson, Charles Proctor, and two other men who had attended the meeting at the Starbuck ranch.

They forded Bear Creek and rode across an almost treeless savannah, Jessie and Bronson in the lead, heading northwest toward Big Meadow several miles away.

Ki, riding in the rear of the group, noted the weapons—sixguns and a few rifles in saddle scabbards—that the men had brought with them. Jessie wore her favorite weapon: a double-action .38-caliber Colt revolver mounted on a .44-caliber frame. It was, he knew, a gun she preferred, despite the fact that its rounds lacked some of the punch of .44-caliber shells, because it had a reduced recoil and allowed her to fire rounds fast and with nearly total accuracy. Bronson wore a two-gun rig, unlike the other men, each of whom wore only a single sidearm. Each loop in his cartridge belt was filled as if he were expecting to go up against an army.

And that's exactly what we're going up against, Ki thought. An outlaw army, never mind how many men happen to have enlisted in it.

Their horses' hooves pounded out a rhythmic tattoo as they crossed the grassy savannah, none of the riders speaking, all of them intent on the task that lay ahead of them—tracking down Pete Damson and the men who rode with him.

After leaving the savannah, they entered a thick forest of shin oaks where there was little sunlight. They weaved among the trees, ducking down to avoid the low-hanging branches of some of the younger trees, and moving more slowly now out of necessity. By the time they emerged from the woods, the sun had disappeared behind a cluster of fair-weather white clouds, bringing some relief to the riders, who had all raised a sweat as they pursued their objective in the heat of the day.

Big Meadow, when they reached it sometime later, was deserted—an unusual condition, since Jessie consistently used it as good grazeland for her stock. The fact that cattle had once grazed contentedly—and safely—in the area was proven by the signs of chewed grass and the charred remains of cookfires built by cowboys herding the cattle.

"Over that way," Jessie said, pointing. "My foreman told me the cattle were driven in that direction. Let's see if we can pick up their trail."

She and Bronson led the way to the northwestern edge of Big Meadow. At first, they saw no sign of any trail. But then, as Jessie and the others rode along the edge of the Meadow, they found the spot where the stock had been driven out of the area. As Wright had said, the ground was torn up, indicating that the cattle had been run hard.

Jessie scrutinized the area carefully from her saddle. She was able to make out the tracks left by four horses traveling behind and on both flanks of the herd that had been rustled.

"It's been a while since they were here," she told the others. "The cattle dug up the ground to a depth where there was some moisture, but most of the tracks have dried up under the sun except for a few here and there. I'd say it was a few hours since Damson was here."

"Which means we've got some hard riding ahead of us," Bronson said, "if we're to catch up with them."

"Let's go," Proctor said bluntly, and spurred his horse into a fast trot, the others riding out behind him.

Two hours later, they came upon a pile of still-moist droppings or "horse chestnuts," as Proctor called them.

"They're not steaming," he observed, "but neither are they dried out, so our quarry can't be too far ahead of us now."

They continued their pursuit, all of them galloping now as they kept their eyes on the horizon ahead, which was cut in places by stark buttes and tall stands of timber.

Jessie suddenly yelled, "They're straight ahead!"

"I don't see a thing," one of the men yelled back.

Jessie pointed at the horizon.

"Those are clouds," the same man said, puzzled. "What—"

"They're not clouds," Ki said as he moved his mount up to the front of the group. "That's dust you're seeing. Trail dust."

They all saw that it was true a few minutes later as they rode on and were able to see the four riders driving the herd of Starbuck cattle ahead of them.

As they drew closer to the outlaws, one of Bronson's guns cleared leather and he fired a snap shot at the men riding ahead of him behind the herd. The shot went wild, but it caused all four men to return the fire as they continued galloping away from their pursuers. Bronson's horse screamed as one of the rounds creased its left shoulder. Bronson fought for control of the horse, which reared as a result of its wound and screamed again. He finally managed to get it under control.

The vigilantes were now firing steadily at the men with the herd and those men, having circled their horses and dismounted, were firing a fusillade of shots in return. Gunsmoke, acrid and thick, filled the air as Bronson, Jessie, and the others were forced to scatter in the face of the fire they were taking.

Like the outlaws, they too dismounted and took cover. Ki found himself not far from where Jessie had taken cover behind a crumbled pile of frost-cracked boulders.

"Stay down," he called out to her from behind the deadfall where he lay sprawled, his horse mingling with the others behind the skirmish line the other vigilantes had formed as they continued firing on the outlaws, none of whom were now visible. But their guns were. They appeared from behind the thick trunks of trees and from the ruins of a cabin that was little more than a pile of rotting timber.

Jessie, both hands on her gun, squeezed off a shot, and saw with satisfaction that it knocked the gun out of the hand of one of the unseen rustlers and sent it flying through the air to fall to the ground some distance away. She smiled grimly.

In the near distance, she could see Bronson and one of the other vigilantes, a farmer named Butler, reloading their weapons. For a moment, the surrounding area was quiet. None of the vigilantes were firing, and neither were the outlaws. In the eerie silence, the sun emerged from the clouds to bathe the land in golden light.

Then, suddenly, a single shot rang out, sounding overloud as it broke the silence. Another one quickly followed it.

Ki frowned. Who were the rustlers shooting at? He quickly discovered that it was not a question of who the outlaws had fired at, but a question of *what* they had fired at. And that *what,* he now saw, had been the herd of approximately fifty head of Starbuck cattle they had stolen.

A third shot sounded.

The cattle, which had been in a mill, raised their heads as one of their number fell dead, shot in the heart. They bawled their dismay and distress. One of them began to run. It was quickly followed by a second, and then by a third.

Another shot from an outlaw gun broke the stillness. It sent the herd into a full-fledged stampede.

Ki scrambled to his feet as the cattle came racing in the direction of the vigilantes' position, their hooves pounding the ground so hard that it shook. He ran to where Jessie was also rising. He seized her by the hand and half-dragged her away from the spot toward which the cattle that had been stampeded by the rustlers were headed.

"Run!" he yelled to the others as he and Jessie fled.

His warning had been unnecessary. Bronson, Proctor, Butler, and the other vigilante were racing out of the way of the oncoming herd.

"Up!" Ki shouted as he and Jessie reached a tall shin oak. He gripped her by the waist and boosted her so that she could grab the lowest branch of the tree.

When she had pulled herself up onto the limb, he leaped up, grabbed hold of it with both hands, and swung himself up beside her. "You okay?" he asked her.

She nodded and then gasped.

Ki looked in the direction she was staring as the herd thundered closer to them, and saw the fourth vigilante, a man named Bender, stumble and fall. They watched Bender's gun fly from his hand and skid along the ground. They saw him struggle to his feet and begin to run again.

But he had lost precious seconds, and during that time the herd had narrowed the distance between him and them. Bender's eyes widened in fear as he saw them bearing down upon him. He increased his pace.

Jessie took aim and fired a round. It ripped into the brain of the lead steer, dropping it in its tracks. The steers behind it stumbled over its body, but then raced on.

Jessie's maneuver had failed. She closed her eyes tightly in order not to see what Ki could clearly see: Bender go down under the thudding hooves of the herd and disappear from sight.

When Jessie found the courage to open her eyes again, the herd had passed on, and all that remained of Bender was a scattered pile of bloody broken bones and ragged bits of cloth that had once been his clothing. Even his gun was battered, its barrel bent by the relentless hooves of the stampeding steers.

"They're gone," Ki said as he scanned the countryside in search of the rustlers. "They took off while we were trying to get out of the way of the trouble they started."

He dropped down from the tree, and then helped Jessie climb down to the ground. They were joined by Bronson, Butler, and Proctor. All of them stood staring at what was left of Bender in silence until Jessie finally spoke.

"Now we have more reason than ever to run those devils to ground. Cattle—that's one thing. Killing one of us—that's another matter altogether."

"And one that demands vengeance," a bitter Bronson muttered.

"They'll get it, if it takes my last breath to give it to them," Proctor declared, his eyes afire.

"Let's go hunt them down," Butler suggested. "We're wasting time standing around here."

They retrieved their horses, and were soon on the trail again. They had ridden less than a mile when they discovered that the trail they were following branched off into two trails.

"They split up," Ki observed. "Two of them went west, two of them north."

"We'll do the same," Jessie declared decisively. "Mel, Ki, and I will head north. You, Proctor, and Butler take the western trail. We'll meet back here later. After we've caught our quarry."

If we catch our quarry, Ki thought. Then he rode out with Jessie as the other three men turned their mounts and headed in a westerly direction.

"At least we don't have to follow a cold trail," Ki observed as they rode on together. "This one's hot as a pistol that's been in a war."

It was true. The trail left by the two rustlers was easy to follow. The grass that had been trampled by horses' hooves had not yet had time to spring back. The occasional broken twig on shrubs they passed had not yet had time to heal. Jessie, who had holstered her revolver, kept her hand on its butt as her mount galloped along beside Ki's.

They rode through a grove of alders and then out onto a rolling plain, where they topped and descended one hummock after another as they continued their pursuit. The clouds had vanished from the sky and the sun burned down upon them with a vengeance.

They were just entering a canyon when the first shots rang out. They wheeled their horses and headed back the way they had come. But they never made it out of the canyon. A fusillade of shots halted them and forced them to take cover. They dismounted and hunkered down behind some boulders.

"Those shots—they came from up there," Ki said, pointing to a ledge halfway up the canyon's eastern wall that was in thick shadow. "It's a good position to ambush somebody from. It's also a good spot from which to keep us pinned down."

Jessie made no comment, unless the two rounds she fired in rapid succession were a comment. Both struck the canyon wall near where the outlaws' shots had come from. Both sent stone dust flying into the air.

Ki looked around him, and then ducked down as a round plowed into the boulder he was crouching behind.

"Are you hit?" an anxious Jessie asked him.

"Nope. But I felt the breeze that bullet just stirred up."
He continued examining his surroundings as Jessie reloaded,

thumbing cartridges out of her gunbelt and inserting them in the empty chambers of her Colt's cylinder.

"Stay here, Jessie, and cover me," Ki said after a moment.

"Where are you going?"

"Up there." Ki pointed to the mesa at the top of the canyon wall. "Then—down there." He pointed to a spot near the far end of the canyon where it narrowed into a gooseneck shape. "Then—over to the other side. I think I can take those two opposite us by surprise."

"Be careful."

Ki eased out from behind the boulder that had provided him cover and, keeping his head low, rounded a rock outcropping and then began to make a hand-over-hand climb. It was hard going, but he kept at it, his head tilted back as he kept his eyes on his goal—the mesa far above him.

When his foot slipped and he slid downward, he grabbed frantically at the sides of the almost sheer wall to keep himself from falling onto the jagged rocks below. He had slipped almost a foot when he managed to ram his right foot into a shallow depression in the side of the canyon wall and simultaneously get a good grip on a slight outcropping of rock just above his head. He hung there for a moment, sweating and desperately hoping that he could hold on. He pressed the side of his face against the canyon wall and remained motionless for a moment before slowly, gingerly resuming his climb.

From below him came the sound of gunfire, but he dared not look down because he suffered from vertigo and looking down, he was certain, might cause him a fall from the dizziness that such a view would instantly inflict on him. He thought of the hot-air balloon he had ridden in with Jessie. This climb was as bad. No, worse.

But he persevered, and sometime later his fingers reached over the rim of the canyon that seemed to soar almost to the sky. He hauled himself over it and onto the mesa that lay baking in the sun.

He rose at once and went racing down toward the far end of the canyon. Once he reached it, he hesitated only a

46

moment and then, backing up several yards, he made a run for the edge of the gorge. He leaped from it and soared out into the air, landing with a body-jarring thud on the other side of the chasm a moment later.

He rose and raced back in the direction he had just come, until he was positioned directly above the two armed men in their rocky eyrie halfway up the canyon wall opposite the lower spot where he could see Jessie crouching. He reconnoitered the rocky wall below him and then began to descend it, practicing the skills he had used in his climb but in reverse. This time, instead of looking down, which he dreaded doing, he was forced to use his feet to feel for purchase in the wall of the canyon, which took time. But it was a procedure that ultimately worked. He descended a foot, six inches, another foot . . . .

Finally, he was forced to look down to establish his position relative to that of the two gunmen he was stalking. He fought off the dizziness that momentarily blurred his vision and made his head swim.

There they were—about twenty yards below him and slightly to the left. Also below him was his goal—a shallow indentation in the wall's rock face which would afford him a place from which to launch the attack he was planning. He braced himself, drew a deep breath, and continued his perilous descent.

He had no sooner done so than his right foot dislodged some loose stones, which went tumbling down the side of the canyon wall. Instantly, he increased the pace of his descent, knowing that the two men below him would look up at the sound of the gravel as it clattered its way down the rock face.

They did.

"What the hell," one of them yelled. "We've got a god-damn mountain goat after us, Billy!"

"Shoot the sonofabitch, Sam!"

Ki scurried like a beetle down the side of the canyon wall, and had just managed to flatten himself against the indentation that was his goal when a shot went whining past his ear. He hugged the wall, his back pressed against it. He

47

knew he had to act and act fast. If he didn't, he would be pinned down where he was exactly as Jessie was on the far side of the canyon.

He was about to make his move when one of the outlaws fired a second shot at him that also missed—but barely. Ki remained where he was, afraid to move, afraid if he did he was dead.

Two shots rang out. They had come from the other side of the canyon and they had the effect—one Ki was sure Jessie, who had fired them, had intended—of forcing both outlaws to drop down behind the rocks that sheltered them. The instant they did so, Ki leaped from his shelf on the canyon wall and landed beside both men.

They let out startled yells as they took aim at Ki. He sent his right leg slashing outward, parallel to the ground, and kicked the gun out of the hand of one of the outlaws. Before his foot had returned to the ground, his left hand rose and chopped downward, slamming into the other's wrist and forcing him to drop his sixgun.

Ki retrieved both weapons and held them on the two men, who were cursing loudly as they damned him to everlasting torment and worse.

"We're climbing down out of this eagle's nest," he told them, ignoring their epithets. "You first. Then you. I'll be right behind you, so don't try anything stupid."

The two rustlers eyed the guns in Ki's hands and then, grumbling, began to obey his order. The one in the lead climbed over a pile of rocks and felt for a footing before starting down.

But the other suddenly threw himself at Ki, who had his guns trained on the descending rustler. He seized Ki's left wrist, savagely twisted it, and then when Ki, fighting back, refused to relinquish the gun in his hand, slammed Ki's hand against the rocky wall of the canyon.

The instant the gun fell from Ki's hand, the rustler scooped it up from the ground. As he did so, his partner picked up a loose rock and flung it at Ki. The rock struck Ki in the right temple, momentarily stunning him and giving the partner enough time to wrest the other revolver from his hand.

The partner began to laugh in a barking fashion as he held his gun on Ki, and the other rustler did the same.

"Ain't this a fine kettle of fish, though?" he crowed. "I was always good at turning tables."

Ki, his temper smoldering as he damned himself for letting these two outlaws get the drop on him, remained silent.

"You want to do the honors, Billy?" the simpering rustler asked.

"Why don't we both plug him, Sam? The more holes we put in him the surer we'll be that he's a dead duck."

"One for the money," Sam chanted. "Two for the show—"

"Three to get ready," a grinning Billy added, continuing the chant that accompanied a children's game.

"And four to go!"

Jessie's words, spoken from behind and just below the the rustlers, took all three men by surprise.

Ki felt relief flood through him as she stepped into sight, her cocked Colt in her hand.

"Give my friend your guns," Jessie ordered, her voice harsh.

When both outlaws had reluctantly done so, she said, "Move out, both of you."

She let the pair pass her, and then as Ki joined her, the rustlers' guns once again in his hands, she made her way down along a winding ledge that led to the ground.

"Where are your horses?" Jessie asked the men she had captured once they reached level ground.

Sam pointed to what appeared to be a solid, brush-covered wall. Ki went to it, and pulled aside some of the brush to reveal the entrance to a kind of cove in the wall where two horses stood quietly browsing. He moved them out, and Jessie ordered their owners to mount up, which they obediently did, their eyes shifting from her to their guns in Ki's hands.

While she waited, Ki went and got their horses. When they were both in the saddle, he and Jessie moved the outlaws out, riding close behind them.

"I'm sure glad you showed up when you did," he told Jessie. "For a while up there, I thought I was a goner."

"You know I wouldn't let you down. I watched you climb down and I saw you get control of the situation—and then lose it."

Ki lowered his head slightly in embarrassment.

"Nothing to be ashamed of," Jessie consoled him. "It's always tricky dealing with sidewinders. Just about the time you think you've got the upper hand they sink their fangs into you. Anyway, as I was saying, when I saw what had happened I decided to lend you a hand."

"I'm mighty glad you did."

"Do you recognize those two?" Jessie asked, indicating the two rustlers riding ahead of them.

"I do. They're part of Pete Damson's gang."

"I figured as much. Damson and the other one— probably Mel and the others have rounded them up by now."

But Jessie and Ki found no sign of Mel Bronson or the two men who had ridden out with him when they reached the agreed-upon spot for their rendezvous.

"Do you think maybe something's gone wrong?" an uneasy Jessie asked twenty minutes later as they found themselves still waiting for Bronson and the other vigilantes to show up.

Before Ki could answer her question, they both heard the sound of horses coming their way. Within minutes, Bronson, Proctor, and Butler rode into sight behind one of the rustlers.

"I see you did better than we did," Bronson declared. "We only got one. This fellow's named Pritchard. His boss—Pete Damson—gave us the slip."

"Three out of four's not a bad score," Ki commented.

"We'll get Damson another day," Jessie said. "Now we have to finish what we started here."

"You're right," Bronson said. "Proctor, Butler—you boys ready?"

"Wait a minute," Jessie said as Proctor and Butler dismounted and both men removed the coiled ropes hanging from their saddlehorns. "What are you planning to do, Mel?"

"Why, hang these three, that's what."

"Hang them? I thought we were going to take them into town and turn them over to the law."

Bronson frowned. *"We're* the law now, Jessie. I thought you understood that,"

"I didn't," Ki said sternly.

Bronson ignored him, his eyes on Jessie's face. "That's why we formed the Vigilance Committee in the first place," he said, speaking with exaggerated patience as if he were explaining the situation to a child. "We agreed that the law was next to useless around here and that we had to do something to replace it. Well, we did and now it's time to carry out the sentence."

"These men haven't had a trial," Jessie protested.

"They don't need none, Miss Starbuck," Butler said as he uncoiled his rope and fastened a honda at one end of it. "They're guilty as sin and we all know it."

"We caught them red-handed," Butler pointed out. "There's no doubt they're guilty."

"So they have to hang," Butler declared as he formed a noose in his rope. Then he went to a nearby post oak and tossed the other end of his rope over a low limb.

"You can't do this, Mel," Jessie argued. "You can't take the law into your own hands."

"Can't I? Watch me, Jessie. You're the one that seems to be having difficulty taking the law into your own hands now that push has come to shove. I thought you understood the function of a Vigilance Committee and the vigilantes who compose it. We're the law, Jessie, and the enforcers of the law. It's that simple."

"Murder's never simple," Ki interjected.

"This is not murder, mister," Proctor declared. "It's justice, pure and simple."

"Simple, maybe," Jessie said, "but far from pure."

Bronson gave her a disgusted look, and then he took his rope from his saddlehorn and proceeded to fasten a noose.

"Lady," the rustler named Pritchard began, "you ain't going to let them do this, are you?"

"It ain't one bit right," the outlaw named Billy blurted out. "You can't be judge, jury, and hangman all rolled up into one. It's against the law."

"You boys sure have developed a healthy if unexpected respect for the law, haven't you?" Bronson taunted them as he threw his rope over another of the post oak's limbs.

"You boys just shut up, hear?" Butler snarled. "If you all went to stand trial—hell, it'd all come down to a necktie party in the end anyway."

"Mel, I don't like this one bit," Jessie protested.

Bronson stopped what he was doing and faced her. "You know these three men were a party to the theft of your stock along with Damson, don't you?"

"Yes, I do but—"

Bronson held up a hand. "You saw them running off the herd with your own two eyes, didn't you?" Before Jessie could object again, Bronson hurried on. "The thing's cut and dried, Jessie. We were all eyewitnesses to what happened. There's no doubt about who committed the crime of stock stealing. *They* did." He pointed an indicting index finger at the three rustlers. "So the logical thing to do is punish them in a way that's fitting."

"And hanging sure is fitting," Butler crowed, an odd bright light in his eyes as he tested the strength of the knot he had made in his noose.

"I don't want any part of this, Mel," Jessie said flatly. "It's more than I bargained for, much more. I thought we were going to apprehend those who committed crimes and then turn them over to the marshal in town. I didn't think this is what the rest of you had in mind."

"I had it in mind right from the start," Bronson told her. "I discussed it with the other members of the Committee and they saw eye to eye with me on the matter."

"And murder's the result," Ki said.

"Call it murder or call it justice," Bronson said offhandedly. "What we're doing is ridding the area of some vermin."

"Not to mention saving the taxpayers some money that would otherwise have to be spent on a trial," Butler declared. "Hell, Miss Starbuck, look at it this way. We're doing the county a favor."

"Don't, Jessie," Bronson said sharply as Jessie's hand dropped to the butt of her holstered gun. He drew his own revolvers and aimed one at Jessie, one at Ki. "If you don't like the tune that's about to be played, I suggest you ride on out of here to a spot far enough away where you can't hear it played or see them dance to it."

Jessie and Ki exchanged glances.

"We ought to at least be given the benefit of clergy," the rustler named Sam whined. "You can't send us to our Maker without somebody says some words out of the Good Book over us first."

"String 'em up," Bronson ordered.

Butler and Proctor saw to it that the nooses were dropped around the necks of the three outlaws. They then tied the free ends of the three ropes to the trunk of the post oak, and tied the hands of the three doomed men behind their backs.

Jessie and Ki rode out without another word.

Behind them they heard one of the outlaws cry out, " 'Yea, though I walk through the valley of the shadow of death, I will fear no evil: for thou art with me; thy rod and thy staff they—' "

His words were suddenly cut off.

Jessie couldn't resist the impulse to turn . . . .

The three bodies hung swaying in the sun at the end of the ropes. She stared at the tree that dared bear such bitter fruit, and then turned away from it and continued her homeward journey, trying and failing to blot out the ugly sight she had just seen.

★

Chapter 4

A week later, as Ki stood at the counter in the Feed and Grain, Hiram Bissett, who ran the establishment, tucked a pencil behind his ear and declared, "If we don't get some rain soon, the drought we're having will wreak havoc on farmers and stockmen alike around here."

"You're right, Hiram," Ki agreed. "What we maybe ought to do is hire us some Indians to do a rain dance for us."

"We had us a drought worse'n this un back in the sixties," said a grizzled old man standing at the counter next to Ki as he picked his teeth with a sliver of wood. "It was so dry then that a fella had to grease his shoes to walk across the parched land else'n he'd get stuck on what little was left of the grass."

"Don't you pay Powell no mind, Ki," Hiram Bissett advised, and clucked his tongue. To the older man he said chidingly, "Dade Powell, you tell the tallest tales in town."

Powell assumed an air of injured innocence. "Why, I tell no tall tales, Hiram, only the gospel truth, so help me, God."

55

"Keep it up, Dade, and you'll get struck by a thunderbolt," Hiram warned.

"That sixties drought," Dade persisted, "it sure scorched the earth. Everything for miles around here and then some was as dry as a Methodist sermon. I remember that time well—like it was yesterday. I also remember what it was like when the rains finally came. You remember that, don't you, Hiram? It was in June—no, July, it was. The sky opened up and we had us a deluge to end all deluges. Before it was over—it rained for nine days in a row that time—we all wished we'd grown fins instead of feet. The rain, it turned the ground as slick as calf slobbers."

Hiram looked at Ki and rolled his eyes.

Ki grinned and proceeded to tally up the bill Hiram handed him. When he had checked the figures, he said, "Put this on Miss Starbuck's account, will you, Hiram?"

"Sure thing, Ki. I hope that new blend of corn and oats will suit your stock. My customers have been saying it's the best they've ever had, bar none."

"Now who's telling tall tales?" Dade Powell sniffed. He winked at Ki. "When Hiram starts into rhapsodizing about the products he's got to sell, it's time you put one hand on your purse and the other one on your hat before you find one or both of them missing. That Hiram—" Powell shook his head and gave the proprietor of the Feed and Grain a sidelong glance "—a man wouldn't dare sleep alongside him with his mouth open if he happened to have a gold tooth."

"Dade," Hiram bellowed, "if you don't get out of here, I'll take a switch to you."

"Watch your temper, Hiram. You don't, you're liable to have a conniption fit or even apoplexy." Dade turned to Ki, a mournful expression on his face. "Don't he beat all, that Hiram? I come in here to pass the time of day and be sociable with him and what happens? He turns mean as a new-sheared sheep."

"Scat!" Hiram hissed.

Dade turned and ambled out of the Feed and Grain.

"That man is a caution," Hiram said, shaking his head as he listed the items Ki had purchased in a green ledger on a page headed STARBUCK.

"Dade's harmless. He just loves to pull a fellow's leg with his stories. I get a kick out of him, to tell you the truth."

Dade's head popped back inside the Feed and Grain. "Ki, I almost forgot. You tell Miss Starbuck old Dade Powell sends his highest regards to her. Will you do that?"

"I most certainly will, Dade."

"She's as pretty as a new-painted wagon with a speckled pup under it," Dade declared. "If I wasn't already hitched—" he sighed "—I'd go courting her, you can bet on that fact."

As Dade's head disappeared from the doorway, Hiram gave a sigh of relief.

"I'll give you a hand, Ki," he said as Ki picked up a sack of grain and slung it over his shoulder.

The two men carried Ki's purchases out to the wagon Ki had waiting, making several trips in the process. By the time they had finished loading the goods into the wagon bed it was almost overflowing. Ki used some rope to lash his purchases in place, and was about to climb up on the driver's seat when he heard his name called.

"Ki, yoo-hoo, *Ki*!"

He looked across the street where the call had come from, and was pleased to see Eudora Paley standing, hands on hips, and smiling at him from the doorway of the Last Chance Saloon. She raised a hand and wiggled her fingers at him.

He returned her wave and then, after bidding good-bye to Hiram, crossed the street and joined her under the overhang fronting the saloon.

"It's nice to see you, honey," he told her, and planted an almost chaste kiss on her right cheek. "How've you been?"

"Fine—but lonesome. You haven't come to visit me in ages."

"I've been busy, Eudora."

She snorted disdainfully. "I have clients who, though they may be as busy as a one-legged man in an ass-kicking contest, can still find the time to spend a sweet hour or two with me."

"I stand properly chastised," Ki replied meekly, suppressing the urge to grin.

"Well, I'll overlook your transgression this time." The implication of Eudora's remark was clear. She clearly would not continue to tolerate being ignored by Ki, who considered himself one of her best customers. Or "clients," as she preferred to call the men with whom she did her lusty business.

"Let's go inside," Eudora suggested. "I just stepped out for a breath of fresh air, but the sun's too hot to suit me."

She took Ki by the arm and led him inside the Last Chance and up to the oak bar. "I'll have a glass of dry vermouth, Harry," she told the bar dog. "What'll you have, Ki? Your usual?"

He nodded at Harry, who proceeded to place a glass of vermouth in front of Eudora and a larger one filled with sarsaparilla in front of Ki.

"To a long life," Eudora toasted, raising her glass and chinking it against Ki's.

They drank.

"You in the mood for some action?" Eucora coyly asked Ki.

"You know me, honey. I'm always in the mood for some action."

"When we finish these—" Eudora indicated their drinks "—we'll go upstairs to my playroom. How's that sound?"

"Heavenly, honey," Ki said sincerely, already beginning to stiffen.

Raised male voices derailed his rousing train of thought. He glanced over his shoulder and saw the men who were gathered around a table that was littered with cards, poker chips, money, and dirty ashtrays. He recognized one of the men: Jerry Talbot, whose brother, Bud, was a close friend of Jessie's.

"Unless I've forgotten how to count," Jerry was saying loudly, "that's the fifth ace you've played this hand, Denby."

The thick-shouldered and barrel-chested older man seated across from Jerry glared at him. He threw down his cards and snarled, "Are you accusing me of cheating, whipper-snapper?"

"You're damn right I am," Jerry answered hotly.

"Let's get out of here," Eudora whispered to Ki. "Before hot words give way to hot lead."

Her words barely registered on Ki's consciousness as he watched the two men confront one another. He knew from past experience that Jerry Talbot had a hair-trigger temper, and by the looks of things, so did the man named Denby he had just accused of cheating him at poker. A volatile combination, Ki was convinced.

"I want my money back, Denby," Jerry declared, reaching toward the pile of folding money and coins that rested in the center of the table.

Denby slammed a fisted hand down hard on the back of Jerry's hand, pinning it to the table. Jerry reacted by cursing vehemently and tearing his hand out from under Denby's. He shot to his feet and went for his gun. But before he could draw it, two of the other players sprang to their feet and seized Jerry.

As Denby's gun cleared leather, Jerry shouted, "I'll kill you, Denby, you cheating sonofabitch!"

"Eudora, you and me'll get together some other time," Ki said without looking at her. Then he was striding across the room to the poker table. When he reached it, he seized the shoulders of the two men holding Jerry.

"Let go of him," he ordered.

The two men looked at him. Whatever it was they saw in his face or had heard in his voice persuaded them to promptly obey the order. They released their holds on Jerry.

"Ki, that bastard there cheated me. Not only was Denby dealing from the bottom of the deck, but he also has a marked deck."

"Jerry, I think it's time you got out of here," Ki said. "Come on, let's leave."

"I'm not leaving," Jerry insisted. "Not till Denby gives me back the money he stole from me with his crooked deck!"

"Get your young friend out of here, mister," Denby growled, addressing Ki. "If you don't, he's going to die."

Jerry tried to vault across the table to get his hands on Denby, but Ki prevented him from doing so. Jerry was yelling at the top of his voice as Ki manhandled him out of the Last Chance. "I'll kill you, Denby. I'll come after you, wherever you might decide to run to, Denby, and when I catch up with you, *I'll kill you!*"

As they went through the batwings, both men collided with Mel Bronson, who had been about to enter the saloon.

"Hey, what—" Bronson spluttered, taking two steps backward to regain his balance.

"Sorry, sir," Ki said. "We didn't see you. I guess we were in too much of a hurry."

"What's all this hot talk about killing?" Bronson asked when he had recovered from his surprise.

Ki explained.

"Calm down, Jerry," Bronson said soothingly when Ki had finished. "That card game you were in isn't the first crooked one and it won't be the last. Shrug it off. Chalk it up to experience."

"I was cheated by Denby," Jerry muttered. "I lost a whole month's pay to him and his rigged deck."

"Maybe that'll keep you at home," Bronson said with a cheerful grin. "Maybe it'll give me a clear field with Janice Drake—at least for the month you're forced to cool your heels for lack of funds."

Ki looked from Jerry to Bronson and back again. "What's that mean?"

"Just that Jerry here and I are romantic rivals," Bronson explained. "We both have our eyes on the same gal—Janice Drake."

"I see," Ki said at the same time that Jerry said, "Let me go, Ki. I want to go back in there—"

"You're not going back in that saloon," Ki said firmly. "Mr. Bronson, if you'll excuse us, Jerry and I will be heading out of town."

"No," Jerry began.

"Yes," Ki said, and marched him down the street. "Where's your horse?" he asked as he returned Bronson's farewell wave and the cattleman shouldered his way though the batwings and into the Last Chance Saloon.

"Right back there where we were—in front of the saloon."

Ki marched him back, and stood by while Jerry freed a roan from the hitch rail and climbed aboard it. "Wait for me. I've got that wagon parked over there in front of the Feed and Grain. We can ride along together."

Ki got his wagon and moved his team out. Jerry took up a position on the driver's side of the wagon with evident reluctance.

"You could have got yourself killed back there," Ki commented after they had traveled for about a mile in silence. "You know that, don't you?"

"I know that. But you're missing the point."

"Am I?"

"The point is I could have killed Denby, the cheating sonofabitch."

"But if he'd drilled you before you could do the same favor for him, what would Miss Janice Drake have to say, do you think?"

Jerry, his jaw set, rode on without answering for a moment, his hands tightly holding the reins. Then, with a shy glance and a grin at Ki, he said, "I like to think she'd mourn me."

"Oh, Jerry had cooled off by the time I left him at the cutoff to his place," Ki told Jessie that evening after he had arrived home, unloaded the wagon, and put the team away.

"Sometimes I worry about Jerry Talbot," Jessie said thoughtfully. "Ever since he and his brother, Bud, and I were kids, Jerry was always the daring one, the reckless one. Did I ever tell you about the time we were out by McKendrick's pasture and Jerry decided he was going to be a bullfighter when he grew up and move to Mexico to practice his new profession?

"McKendrick's prize bull was in the pasture, and I suppose that's what gave Jerry the idea, absurd as it was—at least at that time. Either that or he just decided he was going to impress the rest of us kids who were with him at the time. Jerry was like that—a rod always ready to attract lightning.

"Anyway, he proceeded to climb over the fence and step down into the pasture. Some of us tried to stop him from doing so, but there was no stopping Jerry Talbot once he got an idea into his head. Secretly, I suspect, we were all actually eager to see what he was going to do next. I don't think any of us thought there was any real danger."

"Full-grown bulls are a real danger under the best of circumstances," Ki offered.

Jessie nodded and continued. "Well, there was Jerry inside McKendrick's pasture and there was the bull over on the far side of it. 'Hey, *toro*!' Jerry yelled. I can hear him now in my memory as clearly as I did in reality that day. 'Hey, *toro*!'

"The bull looked at Jerry and Jerry did a little dance, using a handkerchief he had taken from his pocket as if it were a bullfighter's cape. He waved it at the bull, and then he picked up a stick on which he draped his handkerchief in the way of a matador—who, as you know, carries not only a sword in the bullring but also a stick on which he drapes a small piece of scarlet silk, the *muleta*.

"We called to Jerry and told him he'd better get out of the pasture while the getting was good. But he stayed where he was, waving his *muleta* at the bull. Slowly at first, and then more swiftly until the animal, which must have weighed close to a ton, was running. Its head was down and there was hellfire in its eyes. To me, as a young girl at that time, it looked like the bull was going to trample Jerry to death. I cried out to him—screamed, actually—for him to leave the pasture.

"But Jerry dodged the bull's thrust and continued yelling, 'Hey, *toro*!' and *'Here, toro, here!'* It was then that the bull wheeled sharply and lunged at Jerry. I swear the bull would have gored and quite possibly killed him if Jerry hadn't stumbled."

"What happened then?"

"The bull, for some reason, sidestepped Jerry where he lay on the ground, the wind knocked out of him, its horns swinging safely past him."

"I hope by that time Jerry had enough sense to get out of a place he didn't belong."

"He did. He jumped up and threw away his *muleta* and ran toward the fence where the rest of us were standing and watching, unable to speak or even move, we were all so frightened. He had almost reached it when he fell again. Oh, I forgot to mention that the bull was chasing him by that time. I finally found my voice again. I screamed a second time and covered my eyes. I couldn't bear to look, to see what I was sure was about to happen.

"Then, as the other kids suddenly started to cheer, I opened my eyes and what do you think I saw?"

"Tell me."

"Jerry's brother, Bud, had vaulted over the fence and was racing toward his brother. When he got to him, he grabbed him and threw him over his shoulder and then ran like the wind. When he got to the fence, he threw Jerry over it, and then he leapt over it just as the bull came crashing into it and almost broke out of the pasture."

"Just in the nick of time."

"Yes, indeed."

"That, I suppose, ended Jerry Talbot's budding career as a bullfighter."

"No, I'm afraid it didn't. Not right away. Jerry wanted to go back and get his *muleta* and try again. I thought Bud was going to kill him. He slapped him once and then punched him in the stomach in an effort to pound some sense into him. Ultimately, Jerry refrained from any more bullfighting that day because Bud threatened to brain him if he ever did anything that foolish again."

"Mel Bronson better be on his toes insofar as Jerry Talbot is concerned," Ki commented.

"What do you mean?"

"While Jerry and I were with Bronson, Bronson told me he and Jerry were courting the same young lady these days."

"Yes. Janice Drake."

"Oh, you knew about that."

"You know how people gossip. Yes, I'd heard about it. Speaking of Mel," Jessie said, her face darkening, "there's been another hanging."

"There has? When? I hadn't heard—"

"This afternoon while you were in town. Mel and some of his vigilantes hanged Darcy Ellwood. You know Darcy, I believe."

"He lives—lived—out on Deep Hollow Road, right?"

"Yes. With his family."

"As I recall, he had quite a brood."

"Eleven children," Jessie said with a sigh. "The oldest's eighteen and the youngest is six months. His wife, Lilly, has been ailing."

"No wonder. She must be worn out with birthing."

"It's more than that, but that's probably a factor. She's got consumption."

"What was Darcy hanged for?"

"Stealing. He was caught inside the mercantile in town in the middle of last night. He had a gunnysack stuffed with food. Darcy hasn't been working much lately. He's fond of the bottle, as you may have heard."

Ki said nothing.

"He said, when he was caught, that he had no food in the house and no money to buy any with. He said his kids were hungry. He said he couldn't stand to look at Lilly of late, the way she was wasting away before his eyes. I understand that one of the vigilantes, a man named Pearce, told him that was no excuse for theft. The next thing anybody knew somebody had a rope and somebody else dragged Darcy to a tree. . . ." Jessie shrugged.

"He did commit a crime," Ki pointed out.

"I know he did. I'm not denying that. It's just that—just that . . ." Jessie's words trailed away.

"It's just that it's wrong to hang a man without a fair trial no matter what he's done," Ki said softly.

Jessie glanced at him. "It's that. It's also more than that. Darcy was a broken man. I don't know what it was that broke him, but I do know he was broken. The only way he could stop the pain he was feeling was to drink, and so drink he did. You don't hang a man like that. If you're the least bit neighborly you lend him a hand, him and his family."

Jessie got up and began to pace back and forth, her hands clasped behind her back. "The vigilantes said they wanted to make an example out of Darcy. They said they wanted what they did to him to serve as a warning to anyone else who might decide to commit the crime of theft."

"A pretty harsh warning, I'd say."

Jessie stopped pacing as a knock sounded on the door. She went to it and opened it. "Bud! This is a surprise. Come in, come in."

"I'm sorry to bust in on you like this without no warning, Jessie," Bud Talbot said as he came, hat in hand, into the house. "Evening, Ki."

"How are you, Bud?"

"No use complaining, as folks say."

"Sit down, Bud," Jessie said. "Would you like some coffee? Something stronger?"

Bud hesitated. "I could use a snort of something, if you've got it, Jessie."

"Whiskey? Bourbon?"

"Whiskey would do nicely."

Jessie went to an inlaid wood cabinet, opened it, and took out a bottle and a glass. She poured whiskey from the bottle into the glass and handed it to Bud before taking a seat opposite him.

Bud downed the drink and put the glass down. He wiped his lips with the back of his hand. "I was just passing by, Jessie. Saw you were still up and thought I'd drop by to say howdy."

"I'm glad you did, Bud. We were just talking about you and Jerry. I was telling Ki about the time when we were kids and Jerry decided to practice bullfighting in the middle of McKendrick's pasture."

Bud almost smiled. "Jerry always did have a way of getting himself in a peck of trouble of one kind or another," he remarked ruefully. "By the way, Ki, I want to thank you for cooling Jerry down in town today. He had, he told me, killing on his mind where that gambler Denby was concerned. If he'd blown a hole in the man, the vigilantes would have had him strung up by now."

When Bud glanced at her, Jessie lowered her eyes.

"Their ropes are seeing a lot of action these days," Bud went on. "You hear about how they went and strung up Darcy Ellwood?"

"Yes," Ki said as Jessie nodded, her eyes still lowered.

"That was a shame, if you ask me. Darcy's had himself a rough row to hoe and that's a fact. I heard you weren't at the necktie party, Jessie."

"No, Bud, I wasn't."

"How come, if you don't mind my asking?"

"No one asked me to participate. That may be because I don't hold with some of the actions or attitudes of the Vigilance Committee and have made my sentiments known to Mel Bronson among others."

Ki noticed that Bud seemed to slump in his chair. With relief? Fatigue?

"You're against them, are you, Jessie, that gang Mel Bronson's leading?"

Jessie frowned and answered, "I'm not sure that's quite the way to put it, Bud. There has been a great deal of crime in this area of late, and most of it, as you no doubt know, has gone unpunished. Something had to be done."

"But is that something what Bronson and his boys are doing?" Bud persisted. "I mean, stringing up any and every evildoer they can get their paws on?"

"No, Bud, I think that's wrong. When I first met with Mel and the others and we decided to form a Vigilance Committee, I was very enthusiastic about what we had done. I felt strongly that some force was needed to counterbalance the forces of disorder that were loose in the land. I thought our committee could be that force since the law as represented by the marshal and his deputies didn't seem capable of doing the job that desperately needed doing.

"Then, when Mel and the others announced they were going to hang those three rustlers that were riding with Pete Damson—you heard about that affair?"

Bud nodded, his eyes fastened on Jessie's face as she continued speaking.

"I objected."

"Strongly," Ki interjected. "But Mel and the others had guns and they weren't very discriminating about who they were willing to turn them on that day."

Bud's eyes never left Jessie's face, but it was clear that Ki's words had registered with him.

"I tried to talk Mel and the others into taking those three rustlers to the marshal, but they wouldn't hear of it," Jessie said, "They argued that the men were guilty of stealing stock, and that was the truth. They were. I saw them driving the stock they stole from me. They didn't deny stealing it. So Mel insisted that the thing to do was mete out summary justice. Ki and I left. They did what they had intended to do; they hanged the rustlers."

"Jessie, I can't tell you how glad I am to hear you say what you just did," Bud said, sitting up straight in his chair. "When I made up my mind to come here tonight, I told myself this was my last chance. I knew it might not work out. But now, after listening to all you've had to say, I know I did the right thing."

"Bud, I'm not following you. Have I missed something?"

"No, Jessie, you haven't. Well, maybe you have. What I mean is, did you hear about the murder of that gambling man named Denby?"

Jessie gave Bud a blank stare as Ki said, "That was the man your brother, Jerry, claimed cheated him in the poker game in town this afternoon. The man he was on the keen edge of killing until I stepped in."

"That's right, Ki," Bud declared. "Well, Denby's dead. He was shot to death tonight."

Jessie gasped. "You mean Jerry did kill him after all?"

67

"No!" Bud's word exploded in the quiet room. He shook his head vehemently. "Jerry didn't kill nobody. Certainly not Denby. But folks are saying he did. That he must of. That him and Denby was sworn enemies. Folks heard about the card game in the Last Chance Saloon. They heard how Jerry said he was going to kill Denby if he ever got the chance on account of how he claimed Denby had cheated him out of a month's pay. Now that Denby's been shot to death, there's those are saying he killed Denby just the way he vowed he would."

"How do you know he didn't do it?" Ki asked in an even tone.

Bud glared at him. "Jerry's no killer. He talks a lot. He's like a barnyard bantam rooster. He's got to strut his stuff. Talk big and loud. Make believe he's a man though he's just a boy at heart still, even though he's full-growed. I know my brother. He wouldn't kill anybody. He's hotheaded but he's no murderer."

Bud's eyes pleaded with Jessie. "You've known the both of us since the time we was tads. You know neither one of us is the killing kind. Jessie, I didn't come by tonight just to say howdy like I claimed awhile back. I came to ask you to help Jerry."

"Help Jerry? How? What do you mean, Bud?"

"Those vigilantes are out after him, Jessie. Bronson's leading the pack and they mean to run Jerry down like he was a fox and they was hounds. If they do, you know Jerry's a goner. They'll hang him high. Jessie, don't let them do that."

Jessie, startled at the abrupt turn events had taken, couldn't speak for a moment. "Bud, maybe you should take Jerry to Marshal Collins. Have him stand trial for Denby's murder. If he's innocent as you claim—"

"No!" Bud cried, and sprang to his feet. He went to the window and peered out into the darkness. "How long do you think he'd last in that flimsy jail in town?" He spun around to face Jessie. "Not as long as a wax cat in hell, that's how long! Bronson and his boys'd raid the place and drag Jerry out and hang him faster'n a stuttering man can say shucks.

68

Jessie, if you were to hide him here, they'd never find him. Nobody'd think of looking for him here. Not in the home of a member of their very own Vigilance Committee."

"Bud, I don't think—"

Bud crossed the room and knelt in front of her. Taking her hands in his, he pleaded, "I couldn't believe you would be as hungry for hangings as the rest of that bunch. I thought I'd come here to sound you out. You let on just now that you're not like the rest of those vigilantes. Was that a lie you told me, Jessie?"

"No, Bud, it wasn't. But—"

"Then take Jerry in, Jessie, and hide him. When things die down some, I'll take him away from here. I'll sell the homeplace and me and my brother, we'll ride. We'll ride far from here where nobody knows us and no rope's waiting for Jerry. We just need time, Jessie. You could give us that time. I'm asking it in the name of friendship's sake. We was always friends, you and me and Jerry. Even though you was born among the high and mighty and we was whelped amongst a bunch of dirt-poor farmers, you always treated us almost like we was some of your own family, so I hoped—"

"Where is Jerry?" Jessie asked, interrupting. "I want to talk to him before I decide what to do."

"He's right outside. Waiting to see if you'll take him in. I'll go call him." Bud rose, went to the door, and opened it. He placed two fingers in his mouth and whistled shrilly.

Almost at once, a rider came into view as he emerged from the trees that served the Starbuck ranch as a windbreak on the north. He drew rein when he reached the house, dismounted, and hurried inside.

Jessie was shocked by Jerry Talbot's appearance. His face was ashen, his hair disheveled, and his hands trembling.

She rose and went to him. She took his hand, murmured a greeting, and led him to a chair. When he was seated, she said, "Bud told me about what has happened. Jerry, I have a question for you and I want you to answer it honestly. Did you kill Denby?"

"No." The word was a whisper, barely audible. "I didn't kill him—or anybody—ever."

Jessie crossed the room and resumed her seat.

"Where were you when the killing took place?" Ki asked Jerry.

"I was nowhere near where it happened."

"Where did it happen?"

Bud Talbot answered Ki's question. "Out on the Post Road near Tupper's Bend. That's what I was told."

"How did you find out about the killing, Bud?" Jessie asked.

"Billy Cooper come by the homeplace riding hard and sweaty. He said he'd just come from town where everybody was talking about the shooting and about how they thought it must have been Jerry who done it. He come to warn Jerry. You know Billy Cooper, Jessie. He went to school with us."

"Apparently he didn't think the speculation and rumor-mongering about Jerry were true," Jessie observed.

"I didn't do it, Jessie," Jerry insisted. "You got to believe me."

"Why don't you just ride out and be done with it?" Ki asked, causing Jessie to give him a sidelong glance.

"Bud wanted me to at first. But I don't want to leave without I say good-bye to a friend of mine."

"Janice Drake," Jessie guessed.

"She and I have taken to walking out together of late," Jerry said. "We've even talked about how marriage might be in our future. I couldn't leave without seeing her first."

"Where were you when the shooting happened?" Jessie pressed.

"As a matter of fact, I was at the Drake homeplace. I'd gone over there to pay a courting call on Janice. But it turned out there wasn't nobody home. I waited and waited but they never showed up, so after about an hour I headed on home again."

"So you have no alibi for the time of the murder," Ki commented.

"If you mean did anybody see me at the Drakes' place or going there or coming from there, no, no one did." Jerry's features stiffened as he added, "But I was there like I said I

70

was, and that's the plain unvarnished truth of the matter."

"You could turn yourself in," Jessie suggested.

"I was considering that idea," Jerry said, his brow furrowing, "but Bud, he said the vigilantes might try storming the jail to get at me. He thought I ought to hide out. I said maybe you might take me in, so we come here."

Jessie saw the hope flaring in Jerry's eyes as he watched her intently. She glanced at Ki, but his expression was non-committal. She drew a deep breath and said, "All right."

"You mean you'll put Jerry up?" Bud asked eagerly.

"Yes, I will. I don't like the idea but, yes, I will. I still think Jerry ought to go to the law and tell his side of the story." Jessie looked from Bud to Jerry and back again.

Neither brother said a word.

Jessie rose. "You can have one of the guest bedrooms, Jerry."

"I thank you from the bottom of my heart, Jessie, I truly do," he exclaimed. "I'll go and put my horse in the barn and be right back."

When Jerry had gone, Bud crossed the room and embraced Jessie. "I don't know how to thank you for what you're doing. Us Talbots aren't known for being sentimental, but I got to tell you I'm close as can be to tears right this very minute."

Jessie hugged Bud, and then they parted.

"I'll come by tomorrow to see if everything's all right," he told her.

Moments later, Jerry returned.

Bud said, "Don't you make a nuisance of yourself while you're here, Jerry. Pick up after yourself and act like you've got some breeding, you hear?"

Jerry finally managed a full-blown smile as he held up his hands, their palms facing his brother, and said, "I'll be on my very best behavior, Bud. You can bet your boots on that."

★

Chapter 5

"Good day to you, Jessie," Jerry Talbot said early the next morning as he ambled into the kitchen of the ranch and then yawned and stretched, his hands reaching for the ceiling.

"Did you sleep well?" Jessie asked as she put some beef on the stove to boil and took some brown eggs from a crock next to the sink.

"As snug as a bug in a rug. I didn't think I would, being worried the way I have been, but I did. I reckon that's because I felt safe for the first time since I heard the vigilantes were hunting me for the shooting of Denby."

"How do you like your eggs?"

"Scrambled."

Jerry sat down at the table and Jessie poured a cup of coffee for him.

"This is strong as an ox," he commented after tasting the coffee.

"I'm afraid I tend to make it too strong. I like it that way and tend to forget that not everybody else does."

"Oh, don't get me wrong. I'm not complaining. I always liked coffee that was strong enough to stand a spoon straight up in. Is Ki up yet?"

"He rode out early this morning to check the new fence line my hands put in. He's an early riser as a rule."

"I kind of got the impression last night that he didn't believe my claim that I was innocent of killing Denby."

"What makes you think that?"

Jerry drank some more coffee before answering. "The kind of questions he asked. They had a bite to them."

"Ki does tend to dig deeply into anything that interests him. But the fact that he asked you a few sharp questions doesn't necessarily mean that he didn't believe you."

As Jessie set a plate of parboiled beef topped by two fried eggs in front of Jerry, he said, "I'll be glad when Bud can sell the homeplace and we can ride out for a place where we can start life over with a clean slate."

Jessie finished toasting two pieces of brown bread over the flames of the wood stove, put the lid back on, and eased the bread off her toasting fork onto her plate. As she sat down across from Jerry, she said, "I probably shouldn't say this but, well, I'm not so sure that starting over somewhere else is necessarily going to get you the clean slate you speak of."

"What do you mean?"

"What a man does in his life usually, in my experience, dogs his footsteps. To put it another way, you can't run away from some things. Some things have a way of trailing a man no matter where he goes."

Jerry chewed thoughtfully for a moment, his eyes on Jessie, who was buttering her toast, and then he put down his fork. "I'm not turning myself in."

Jessie said nothing.

"They'd drag me out of that jail in town and lynch me for sure. Even if they didn't and I lived to stand trial, I probably wouldn't get a good judgment from the twelve men and true they'd pick to try me. Everybody's already half-convinced I'm guilty. Won't be long before they're altogether convinced."

"I'm sorry, Jerry. I shouldn't have brought it up again. You'll have to do what you think is best."

"I thank you for giving me the opportunity to do that very thing."

"How's the beef?"

"Tasty. Hits the spot, it does."

"I'll be riding out to where we've pastured our stock when I'm finished here," Jessie said after finishing the last of her toast. "I'd advise you stay inside. You don't want anybody to see you, and people do pass by here from time to time."

"I'll make myself scarce, you can count on that. I just hope I don't have to do it too long or I'm liable to wind up with cabin fever."

"A case of cabin fever's a lot better than a fatal case of a stretched neck."

The words were no sooner out of Jessie's mouth than she regretted uttering them because Jerry's face had turned suddenly pale at their harsh meaning.

Ki noted as he rode that some of the posts that supported the new barbed-wire fence had not been sunk deep enough, with the result that they were tilting and the fence was hanging at an angle. Such was the case for a distance of about thirty yards in one section of the fence that climbed a sloping hummock on the edge of the Oak Barrens. It would, he knew, not be hard to find out who had been responsible for that particular stretch of fencing—who had failed to properly sink the posts. Ranch foreman Ed Wright, once informed of the facts, would be able to determine that with little or no trouble.

Ki rode on, his keen eyes scanning the area. There was a bunch of cows down in a hollow that lay like a deep bowl about a half mile from the fence's perimeter. They were almost all down on their bellies in a patch of shade beneath some towering manzanita trees, chewing their cuds and presumably watching the world pass them by. Another bunch ambled along the edge of a stream that flowed through the area. A third bunch stood in the sunlight spilling out of the bright blue sky, not moving so much as a muscle as if paralyzed by the rays of the brassy sun.

As Ki crested a low ridge some time later, he drew rein when he saw the four riders strung out down below him. They were too far away for him to make out their identities, but as he sat his saddle watching them, they suddenly came to a halt. He continued watching as they conferred among themselves and then changed direction and headed toward him.

They had almost reached him when they halted again. By now he was able to recognize them—Mel Bronson and some of his vigilantes.

He watched one of the men, one he whose name he didn't know and whose face he didn't recognize, dismount and lift the left front foot of his mount. The man shook his head and said something to Bronson. When he let go of his gelding's foot, the horse placed it gingerly on the ground. It was at that moment that Bronson noticed Ki atop the ridge. He raised a hand and waved. Ki put heels to his bay and rode down to where the men were gathered.

"Howdy, Ki," Bronson greeted him. "What brings you out this way?"

"Riding fence," Ki replied.

"Is Jessie to home, do you know?" Bronson inquired.

Ki hesitated a moment and then answered, "She was when I left this morning. But she may not be now." He knew why he was hedging. It was because he was sure Bronson and the others were out hunting Jerry Talbot.

Such proved to be the case.

"We're looking for a killer," Bronson declared. "I suppose you heard about Jerry Talbot's shooting of that fellow named Denby."

Ki nodded, but said nothing.

"Nasty business," one of the vigilantes volunteered. "Shot down in cold blood, Denby was."

"Like a dog," added the man with the lame horse.

Ki decided to try to change the subject. "What's wrong with him?" He pointed at the man's gelding.

"He threw a shoe a ways back. His foot's so sore he's not really rideable."

"Ki," Bronson said, "I'd like to ask you a favor on behalf of Jim Bob Simpson here. I'd like to ask you if we could ride over to your place and fire up Jessie's forge and put a new shoe on his horse. Do you think that would be all right?"

Ki knew he couldn't say no. If he did, it would raise suspicions in the minds of the men he was facing. They'd be sure to wonder why he was turning down a purely neighborly request.

"I don't see why not," he finally answered, although he saw very well why these men should not visit the Starbuck ranch at this particular time. The reason was Jerry Talbot's presence there.

"We thank you kindly, Ki," Bronson said. "We were headed in that general direction, so it won't be real far out of our way." Turning to Simpson, Bronson said, "Jim Bob, you climb up behind me and you can lead your horse to the Starbuck ranch."

When Jim Bob Simpson had done so and the men had moved out again, Ki remained where he was, watching them go. Then he rode down the far side of the ridge, raked his bay with his spurs, and sent it galloping along the base of the ridge. He intended to ride north, and then turn his mount and ride parallel to the course Bronson and the others were now taking as they made their way to Jessie's place. He believed he had a good chance of getting there and being able to warn Jerry before Bronson and the others could arrive since Simpson's lame mount would slow them down. He lashed his bay with the reins and galloped on. Sometime later, he changed course abruptly and rode parallel to—but out of sight of—Bronson and his vigilantes.

"That does it," Jessie said as she and Jerry Talbot finished washing and drying their breakfast dishes. "It's time for me to be on my way."

Jerry watched her as she tied a bandanna around the slender column of her neck and then took down from a pegboard on the wall a flat-topped black Stetson with a rawhide chin strap.

Before she could put it on, he crossed the room and took her in his arms. "It's been a long time," he murmured, burying his face against her neck. "Too long a time."

His actions surprised Jessie, but she did not push him away. The feel of his arms around her was a familiar one, although his arms had not been around her for, as he had said, a long time. How long? As he nuzzled her neck, she thought about it, and realized with something akin to shock that she had not made love to Jerry Talbot in over two years.

"It seems like every time I looked you up lately," Jerry murmured, "you were gone somewhere far afield. Once somebody told me you were in Hong Kong, wherever that is."

"I have far-flung business interests," she whispered. "They sometimes require my presence on the scene whether it's across the country or across the world."

"I've missed you, Jessie. I've missed the touch of you, the sweet smell of you, the feel of you in my arms. I can still remember the first time we made love. I was just sixteen—"

"You were seventeen."

"It was in our hay barn."

"It was in your father's apple orchard."

"You were a virgin."

Jessie decided not to correct him on that particular point.

"It was wonderful."

With that she could not argue. Their encounter had been wonderful. She had at the time thought she was in love with the tow-headed, too-tall boy Jerry Talbot had then been. She had thought his eyes were the bluest and most beautiful she had ever seen. Was what she had felt for him then the reason she had agreed to hide him now here in her house so that the vigilantes would not find and hang him? That had, she decided, definitely played a role in her decision.

"If you don't want to—" Jerry began.

Jessie drew back from him and placed an index finger on his lips. Then she withdrew it, took his head between her hands, and kissed him eagerly full on the lips. She offered no objection as his tongue slid between his teeth and then between hers. She allowed it easy entry, and shuddered as it began to probe and Jerry's hands began to roam up and down her body. She pressed her body against his as he cupped her breasts and fondled them.

"Let's go upstairs," she whispered. "To my bedroom."

Jerry was more than willing. He took her by the hand and let her lead him out of the kitchen and upstairs to a room he hadn't seen for years. Not since the second time they had coupled on a sultry summer day when her father, who was then still alive, and all the servants were out of the house.

As she closed the door behind them, he seized and kissed her again, his hands on her hips as he held her pelvis firmly against his own.

She managed to free herself, and then began to undress. He did the same, never taking his eyes off her as he stripped. When they were both naked and lying side by side on the bed, Jerry ran his fingers down between her breasts, and over the slight mound of her belly, and then his hand covered her hot mound. He massaged her. His finger slid into her. She moaned. It slid more deeply into her and then emerged, slick with her juices. He rolled over on top of her and thrust himself into her, his entry made easy by her wetness.

She let out a soft moan as he widened the inverted V of her legs. Then he thrust down hard, and as he did so, her legs encircled him and her arms wrapped themselves around his body. He began to move in a slow steady rhythm, not wanting to rush the matter, intending to pleasure Jessie as much as himself and to fully savor this experience.

Her fingernails dug into his bare back as she too began to move in rhythm with him. "Faster!" she commanded moments later.

He immediately increased the speed of his thrusting in obedience to her command.

She squirmed beneath him, thrusting her body up to meet his own and then sinking back, only to thrust almost violently upward again.

"Are you almost ready?" he asked her hoarsely, knowing that he couldn't—wouldn't want to—contain himself much longer.

"Yes," she whispered breathily in his ear.

"Now!" he said as he buried his face in her sweet-smelling hair.

As he exploded within her, his entire body shuddered for several long seconds before gradually becoming calm again. He lay there rigid within her, his lips gently nuzzling her neck.

Her arms relaxed. She broke the tight circle of her legs and let them drop down upon the bed.

Jerry withdrew from her and flopped over on his back beside her. He put his hands behind his head and lay there staring up at the ceiling.

Jessie raised herself up on one arm and looked down at him. "Was it like old times?" she whispered with a faint smile.

"Better than old times. It was real good new times."

He reached up and stroked her firm breasts. Then he raised his head and teased the nipples of both breasts with his darting tongue.

Jessie responded by reaching down and stroking his softening shaft. In seconds, she had him stiff again. She rose and assumed a sitting position on the edge of the bed. She beckoned to Jerry.

He also rose and, following her instructions, got off the bed and stood facing her, his erection throbbing and pawing the air only inches from her face.

Jessie reached out and ran the tips of her fingers along the length of his shaft. Then she gripped his buttocks with both hands and pulled him closer to her.

Jessie opened her mouth and her lips locked on him.

He stared down at her, drowning in a lake of delight, his hands on his hips, as she closed her eyes and began to suck his shaft. Her head bobbed rhythmically backward and forward until he reached out and clasped his hands behind her head. He began to buck, the sounds of Jessie's wet sucking adding to his arousal, the warmth of her tongue as it laved him inducing ecstasy not only in his shaft but throughout his entire body.

He erupted seconds later. But Jessie did not withdraw from him as she had done in the past. Now she kept her lips locked on him as she swallowed hard several times and his seed continued spurting into her eagerly receptive mouth.

Finally, they separated. Jessie dropped back on the bed, her arms flung out on both sides of her body, her eyes dreamy.

Jerry sat down next to her. "Was it good?" he asked huskily.

She shook her head, disappointing him, and then quickly added, "It wasn't just good; it was grand."

They lay there lazily for uncounted minutes, until at last their reverie was shattered by the sound of the downstairs front door bursting open and Ki calling out at the top of his voice, *"Jessie!"*

Jerry sat up in bed, an expression of mild alarm on his face.

Jessie motioned to him to remain where he was, and went to the bedroom door, which she opened a crack. "Ki, I'm up here."

"Where's Talbot?" Ki yelled from the bottom of the stairs.

"He's here with me. Why?"

"Hide him. Or at least, tell him to stay where he is. Mel Bronson is coming. He has some of his vigilantes riding with him."

"He's coming here? Are you sure?"

"Yes, I'm sure. He'll be here soon. Any minute now, I expect."

"Why is he coming here?"

"One of the men with him has a horse that's thrown a shoe. He wants to nail a new one in its place and he asked me when I ran into him near here if it would be all right to use your barn to do the job in. I had to tell him it *would* be all right. If I didn't, he would have wondered why I turned him down, and who knows what that might have led to."

"I understand. I'll be right down."

Jessie closed the bedroom door and turned to face Jerry. "You heard?"

"I heard."

She noticed that his face had paled. She also noticed the way his upper teeth had begun to worry his lower lip.

"You stay here in my bedroom. I'm going to get dressed and go downstairs. You'll be safe here."

Jessie was sure that Jerry had some doubts about his safety. They were evident in the frown on his face and in his furrowed brow. She hurriedly dressed and then, as Jerry did the same, she kissed him lightly on the lips and left the bedroom. She had no sooner gotten downstairs when she heard the sound of horses outside.

Stomping. A shrill nicker.

She went to the window and looked out.

Bronson. Three men with him, all of whom she knew. She glanced at Ki, who was standing nearby.

"Did they say anything to you?" she asked Ki, her back turned to him.

"You mean did they say anything about Talbot. They did. They said they were out hunting him."

A knock sounded on the front door.

Jessie turned and, squaring her shoulders, went to the door. She affixed a smile on her face as she opened it, and greeted the four men standing outside. "Good morning, gentlemen. I understand one of you has a problem with a lame horse."

"Howdy, Jessie," Bronson said. "I gather Ki's gotten here ahead of us and told you we were coming by. I hope you don't mind the imposition, but we can't track with a lame horse slowing us down. Can we use the forge in your barn to hammer a new shoe on Jim Bob's mount?"

"Of course. Help yourselves, gentlemen."

Jessie was about to close the door when Ki came up behind her and whispered, "I just remembered. Talbot's horse is out in the barn. Stall them long enough for me to get it out of there. If they should see it . . ."

82

Jessie stiffened, but she managed to keep the bright smile on her face. "You men look like you've been riding hard."

"We have," Bronson said, "and that's a fact."

"Why don't you come in and rest for a bit? The sun's hot but I've got some fresh lemonade cooling down in the springhouse. Would you like some?"

Jim Bob Simson licked his lips and glanced at Bronson as Ki slipped out of the room behind Jessie on his way to the back door.

"Well," Bronson said, as the men with him awaited his decision, "I reckon we can take a few minutes off from our tracking. Jim Bob, you go on down to the barn, why don't you, and we'll go inside to where it's cool and take Jessie up on her kind offer of some fresh lemonade."

"I could use some lemonade myself," Jim Bob said. "My horse, I figure he can wait a few minutes while I wet my whistle."

"Come in, gentlemen," a relieved Jessie said as, out of the corner of her eyes, she caught a glimpse of Ki making his stealthy way toward the barn in the distance.

"Now, Jim Bob," Bronson said as the man made a move toward the open door, "I think it'd be best for all concerned if you shoed that horse of yours as fast as you can so we can be on our way again after Talbot. You go take him on down to the barn and I'll send Calvin here down with some lemonade which you can drink while you're firing up the forge."

Jessie's smile evaporated as Jim Bob Simpson dismounted and began to lead his horse toward the barn. "I'll go down to the springhouse, gentlemen," she said as cheerfully as she could manage under the tense circumstances. "You all go on inside an make yourselves comfortable. I'll be right back."

She stood aside to let her unexpected and unwanted guests enter the house, and then hurried after Simpson, who was making his way toward the barn, his horse in tow.

"Jim Bob," she said when she caught up with him, "you wait right here. I'll go get the lemonade and give you some to take to the barn with you."

"I'm obliged to you, Miss Starbuck. I've sweated so much today I feel about as dry as a baked bone."

Jessie hurried to the springhouse, hoping Ki would be able to spirit Jerry's horse away before it was too late. To give him more time to do so, she dawdled inside for nearly five minutes before removing two crocks from the cool water of the stream that flowed through the springhouse and returning to where Simpson stood waiting for her. She handed him one of the crocks and then, carrying the other, started back toward the main house. She glanced over her shoulder once, and saw Simpson tilting the jug up on one crooked arm and drinking deeply from it. She saw no sign of Ki.

She looked up and caught a glimpse of Jerry Talbot peering at her through her bedroom window. She wanted to signal him to move away from the window, but feared doing so in case the vigilantes were watching her from inside the house. She settled for frowning. Her expression evidently conveyed her annoyance to Jerry, because he quickly stepped away from the window so that he could no longer be seen.

Just before entering the house, Jessie glanced again over her shoulder, in time to see Jim Bob Simpson leading his horse into the barn. There was still no sign of Ki.

Once inside, she gathered some glasses and proceeded to pour lemonade for her guests. They accepted her offering eagerly, quickly downing the contents of the glasses and gladly accepting refills.

They were in the process of emptying their glasses for a second time when shouts from outside the house reached them.

Jessie stiffened.

Bronson went to the window and drew aside the curtain covering it. "Now what do you suppose has got into Jim Bob? He looks like he's got a burr in his britches for sure."

Jessie turned. Through the window she could see Simpson standing halfway between the house and the barn. He was waving his arms and pointing at the barn. He beckoned to Bronson, who hurried outside, followed by the others.

"Mel!" Simpson yelled. "He's here. By God in his great heaven, he's here!"

84

"Who's here, Jim Bob?" a puzzled Bronson asked.

"Talbot, that's who."

"Talbot is here?" an incredulous Bronson asked. "Where?"

Simpson, dancing about in his excitement, answered, "I don't know where but he's here somewheres. His horse is in the barn."

Jessie's heart sank as Ki emerged from the barn and gave her a look which conveyed the fact that he had failed to spirit Jerry's horse away before it was discovered by Simpson.

"You sure it's Talbot's horse?" the vigilante Bronson had called Calvin asked Simpson.

"Sure, I'm sure. It's got the Rocking T brand on its shoulder."

"That's Talbot's brand," Calvin told Bronson, who nodded and said, "Simpson, you go search the barn. Look up in the hayloft. We'll search the house."

"You'll do no such thing," Jessie exclaimed. "You have no right—"

"Jessie, you're wrong about that. We've got every right in the world to do whatever it takes to run Talbot to ground. Now, you just step out of the way and we'll be about our business."

"No!"

Bronson signaled to Calvin, who seized Jessie and held her motionless as Bronson and his vigilantes reentered the house.

"Let her go," Ki said as he arrived on the scene.

"Mel wants—"

"I don't give a damn what Mel Bronson wants," Ki snapped. "Let her go, mister. You'll be mighty sorry if you don't, I assure you."

Calvin met Ki's penetrating gaze, hesitated a moment, and then released his hold on Jessie, who went to stand beside Ki.

Both of them listened to the shouts of the men as they searched the house. Jessie's gaze drifted up to her bedroom window. She saw no sign of Jerry. She glanced at Ki, who was also watching the window.

The sound of shattering glass tore through the air then as Jerry leaped through the closed window and landed on the roof, his arms outstretched and waving wildly as he tried to maintain his balance.

Calvin drew his revolver and took aim at Jerry, but Ki reached out and, in one swift sharp movement, knocked the gun from his hand.

"Run!" Jessie cried as Jerry reached the edge of the roof and jumped down to the ground.

Jerry ran, heading for the barn and his horse.

But he didn't get far. Bronson emerged from the house, his gun drawn, and fired. His shots struck Jerry in the back, lifting him inches off the ground. His hands flew up as if he were reaching for the sky—or trying to fly away from the horror that had so suddenly overtaken him.

Jessie was running toward him before he crumpled to the ground. She dropped to her knees beside him and felt for a pulse in his neck. There was one. Faint. Thready.

"Ki!" she cried, tears welling in her eyes. "Get the wagon ready. We've go to get Jerry to the doctor."

Ki sprinted toward the barn.

Behind him, Bronson and the other vigilantes holstered their guns and strode over to where Jessie was still kneeling on the ground and whispering Jerry's name over and over again as tears slid down her cheeks.

"It didn't work," Jerry, his eyes closed, managed to murmur, his words emerging with a frothy mix of saliva and blood. "They found me, Jessie."

"We're going to take you to the doctor," she said, leaning close to Jerry so he would be sure to hear her.

"Too late."

Jessie wanted to take him in her arms. She wanted to hug him as memories of all the good times they had had together raced through her mind.

"Tell Bud—" Jerry's words faded away. "Tell him—*oh, Jessie!*"

His eyes flew open and stared wildly at the sky for a moment, and then the life left them. Jessie saw them glaze.

She saw his mouth go slack as blood continued to ooze from it. She felt his death. It was cold in her arms. She released her hold on Jerry and looked up through tear-washed eyes at Bronson.

"You didn't have to kill him."

"He was running away. You saw that for yourself."

Jessie wanted to fly at the man, strike him over and over again with her fists, claw at his face, his eyes, make him hurt, make him sorry he had stolen the life of her young friend. But she did nothing. She said nothing more. She turned and strode toward the barn.

As Ki emerged from it, leading the team he had hitched to the wagon, she halted and shook her head. "Jerry doesn't need a doctor anymore," she said softly. "We'll take him home."

"What was he doing hiding in your house?" Bronson barked from behind Jessie.

"Exactly that," she responded, spinning around to face her questioner. "He was hiding. So that you wouldn't find and kill him."

"Aha. So you knew he was there."

"Yes, I knew he was there."

"It looks to me, Mel," Simpson drawled, "like the lady didn't want to see justice done."

"Jessie always wants to see justice done," Ki interjected angrily. "What she doesn't want to see done is a clear case of cold-blooded murder."

"Talbot ran to get away from us," Simpson said. "That means, as far as I'm concerned, that he was guilty."

"If he was innocent," Calvin offered, "he wouldn't of had any cause to flee like he did."

"That's preposterous!" Jessie exclaimed. "He had no gun and you men were armed. He knew you had hanged those rustlers. What would you expect him to do under the circumstances—stand his ground and try to convince you he was innocent? He knew he wouldn't stand a chance if he did that."

"It's a clear-cut case of an eye for an eye," Bronson intoned. "Talbot took Denby's life. We took his."

"Now poor Denby can rest in peace," declared Calvin. "He's been avenged."

"Avenged!" Jessie cried, her voice somewhat shrill. "You men don't even know for sure that Jerry Talbot killed a fly, let alone that gambler."

"He swore he was going to kill Denby," Bronson argued. "Your friend, Ki, heard him say so. Isn't that right, Ki?"

"I've got to load Jerry in the wagon," Ki said to Jessie, and proceeded to drive the wagon over to where Jerry's body lay lifeless on the ground.

"I saw Jerry Talbot out on the Post Road last night," Bronson said.

"Which way was he headed?" Jessie asked.

"East."

"He was on his way to Janice Drake's place to pay a call on her."

"Denby was killed on the Post Road last night," Bronson said.

"That's not proof that Jerry Talbot killed him," Jessie protested. "The fact that Jerry was on the Post Road and you say Denby was killed on it—that doesn't prove Jerry killed him."

Bronson shrugged. "Well, gents, our work is finished here. We'd best be on our way."

"I never did get to shoe my horse," Simpson complained.

"I doubt you'd be welcome to do so here and now," Bronson said, "considering the attitude toward our work that Jessie seems to have."

"You're one hundred per cent right on that score," she said sharply. She walked briskly away, heading toward the spot where Ki was loading Jerry's body into the bed of the wagon.

Behind her the vigilantes swung into their saddles and rode away.

Ki brought the wagon to a halt in front of the Talbot homestead. He had no sooner done so than the front door opened and Bud came out.

88

"What's wrong?" he asked, looking from Ki's face to Jessie's. They were both somber.

Jessie found herself desperately wishing she could answer, "Nothing," to Bud's question. She turned her head and looked down into the wagon bed behind her.

Bud approached the wagon, walking slowly, his eyes fixed on her face. He gripped the side of the wagon's bed with both hands and stared down at the body of his brother.

"Who did it?" he asked in a monotone.

Jessie tried to answer him, but found she couldn't speak.

Ki explained to Bud what had happened.

"You mean they shot him down like a dog," Bud snarled when Ki had finished his account of the slaying of Jerry Talbot.

"They seemed to have some notion that they were halting a fugitive from justice," Jessie offered, bitterness tinging her tone.

"A fugitive from *vigilante* justice!" Bud growled, giving the word "vigilante" a sheen of scorn as he spoke the word.

"Bud," Jessie said, "they said—Mel Bronson did—that Denby was found dead on the Post Road. He also claims he saw Jerry on the road the night Denby was shot down."

"So what?"

"So maybe nothing," Jessie said hastily when she saw the anger flaring in Bud's eyes. "I know that Jerry had gone to call on Janice Drake last night and would have traveled along the Post Road to do so. I was wondering—"

"No, Jessie. Jerry didn't kill Denby. I don't care what anyone says. I don't care where he was last night. *He didn't do it!*"

"I'll give you a hand with Jerry," Ki offered. Then, with Bud's help, he removed the corpse from the bed of the wagon and carried it into the house, where he and Bud placed it on a sturdy wooden table in the kitchen.

"I'll have to get some of our relatives to come over to wash and ready the body for burying," Bud said dully, staring down at his brother. "We'll get him into the ground as soon as we can. Tomorrow, if that turns out to be possible. The weather's turned hot again."

"Bud, I'm sorry about what happened," Ki said as he held out his hand. "It's a terrible loss, and I hope you find the strength to bear up under it," he added as the two men shook hands.

"It's not right, Ki. It's just not right, dammit. Jerry was a good man, a decent man. He wasn't a killer."

Ki could think of nothing more to say.

Giving the corpse a forlorn look, Bud accompanied Ki outside.

"I don't know if it will be of any help," Jessie said to Bud, "but I'm going to ride into town and have a talk with Marshal Collins about what has happened. I want to know if the marshal's aware of what Bronson and the men riding with him have been doing and why."

"What good will that do?" a bitter Bud asked as he stared off into the distance.

"I said I don't know that it will help, but it's something I feel I should do."

"As far as I'm concerned, you're locking the barn after the horse has been stolen," Bud commented. He turned to face Jessie. His eyes were cold when he asked, "Are you sure you didn't have anything to do with what happened out at your place today?"

Jessie, shocked, shook her head vigorously. "No, of course I didn't. How can you ask such a thing? How can you even think it?"

"I can think it because you're one of them, Jessie. It was at your house, I was told, where it was decided that you all would form a Vigilance Committee. Which makes you one of the vigilantes. Maybe it wasn't a coincidence that Bronson and his boys came to your place today. Maybe you sent word to them that Jerry was hiding out with you."

"I did no such thing!" an indignant Jessie cried. "I was very fond of Jerry. You know that, Bud."

"I don't know what I know anymore. The world has suddenly turned upside down for me."

90

"Bud, I feel I must tell you that I had nothing to do with Jerry's death. You're wrong in thinking I might have had something to do with it."

"Thank you for bringing Jerry home. I'd best be about the business of making funeral arrangements." Bud turned on his heels and reentered his house.

Jessie glanced at Ki, and then he climbed up on the wagon beside her. After leaving the Talbots' homeplace, they traveled in silence for some time before Jessie said, "The Vigilance Committee is tearing us all apart. You heard what Bud said to me. It's incredible that he thinks I might have had a hand in Jerry's death. This is a bad business, Ki. It's not only the killing I deplore, but also the way it's beginning to turn friend against friend."

Ki agreed with her and said so. Then: "Where are we going?"

"To town."

"To talk to Marshal Collins?"

"Yes. Maybe he'll put a stop to this terrible business when we tell him what happened to Jerry."

★

Chapter 6

"I don't know what you're accusing me of!" Marshal Collins
practically shouted at Jessie as she and Ki sat facing him
across his battered wooden desk.

"Marshal, I'm not accusing you of anything," Jessie
said calmly, almost sedately, in an effort to calm the
volatile man's temper. "I have been merely pointing out
that Mel Bronson and the rest of the members of the
Vigilance Committee are, it seems to me, encroaching
on your domain. I refer, of course, to law enforcement."

"I don't think of it that way, Miss Starbuck," Collins
spluttered.

"How do you think of it, Marshal?" Ki inquired.

"As a help to the more official acts and efforts of the law
as represented by me and my two deputies."

"They've killed five men," Jessie said. "There were the
three rustlers who stole some of my cattle, there was Darcy
Ellwood, who they hanged for theft, and then there was the
murder of Jerry Talbot earlier today. That's five murders
from my point of view."

93

"That's cleansing the countryside of evildoers from my point of view," Marshal Collins countered with something like a smirk.

Jessie found his almost casual attitude toward what she considered the crimes committed by the Vigilance Committee infuriating. She had to make a conscious effort to control her own temper in the face of his, which had already flared twice during their increasingly heated discussion.

"By the way, Miss Starbuck, you've got your facts and figures wrong."

"Marshal?"

"What I mean is, there aren't five men that the Vigilance Committee did in. There's six as of real early this morning."

"Six?" Ki prompted. "Who else did they kill?"

Collins gave him an annoyed glance before answering. "They brought to justice a lone rider named Pete Damson. I reckon you all might have heard of him."

"We've heard of him," Ki said.

"He was the leader of the gang that stole my cattle," Jessie said. "What happened to him?"

"Two of the vigilantes—fellas named Dick Offutt and Junior Dell—ran into him south of town where he was hiding out in an old abandoned soddy. They'd stopped to water their horses at a stream near the soddy when Damson, who must of thought they'd been trailing him—which they weren't—took a couple of potshots at them.

"Well, sir, they took cover in a helluva hurry, as you might imagine, and then they returned the fire. At first, they didn't have the least little idea about who it was they were shooting at. Not until Damson himself yelled something that gave him away. Junior roused me out of bed this morning to tell me about the shootout. He said Damson yelled, 'You ain't never going to take me alive, not Pete Damson, you ain't.' Well, the fact of the matter is, they didn't. Take him alive, I mean."

Collins's smirk was back. "They hung him to a cottonwood growing out that way, and as far as I know, he's hanging out there still."

94

"I take it, Marshal," Jessie said, "you don't intend to do anything to stop this sort of thing."

"Stop it? Of course I'm not going to do anything to stop it. Hell, Miss Starbuck, I applaud it."

"Now, before you go and get your dander up, you just listen up to what I got to say on the subject, and then we can close the books on the matter once and for all. Pete Damson was a rustler, among some other unsavory things. I reckon you don't know he abused the Widow Ransom a few months back."

"No, I didn't know that," Jessie responded.

"We tried to keep the whole thing quiet. For the widow's sake, if you understand my meaning. Word gets out about a thing like that, why, it can ruin a woman's reputation faster'n a dog with fleas can scratch. So like I said, I kind of kept the whole thing under wraps for the widow's sake. But Damson did it. Busted in on her one fine day when she was all alone, threw her down and—well, you can imagine what happened without me saying it right out loud in polite company."

"You're saying he raped her," Jessie said.

"That he did, yep. Anyway, you yourself know that he stole your stock—him and the three other men he had riding with him. So it's not a question of was he guilty or not. He was. Am I right or am I wrong, Miss Starbuck?"

Reluctantly, Jessie answered, "You're right, Marshal."

Collins beamed benignly at her. He folded his fat hands over his paunch and continued. "The vigilantes did the county a favor by ridding us of those four bad boys. As for Darcy Ellwood, he was caught red-handed in the mercantile with a sack full of food he was in the act of stealing. Another guilty one the vigilantes took care of with dispatch. As for Jerry Talbot, that case is not quite so clear."

"There was no proof—none—that Jerry Talbot killed Denby," Jessie pointed out.

"Don't interrupt me, Miss Starbuck. I'm a man with a one-track mind and interrupting me like you're doing, it gets me all mixed up. Now, where was I? Ah, yes, I remember. Talbot was seen by Mel Bronson out on the Post Road last night, which is the selfsame place where Denby's body was found *last night* with enough lead in it to sink a canoe. Now maybe nobody saw Talbot pull the trigger, but everybody knows he meant to kill Denby. Popular opinion has it that he went and did what he intended to do, so nobody's mourning Jerry Talbot's passing much."

"Marshal," Jessie said, suppressing a growing sense of exasperation, "don't you consider yourself a part of the county's judicial system any longer?"

"Sure, I do. Why only yesterday I arrested a fella who snatched a lady's purse right off her arm on Main Street. I caught him and he's back in a cell cooling his heels right now. Why do you ask?"

"Because I believe it's your duty to do what you can to disband the Vigilance Committee so that no more crimes can be committed by its members."

"I've got no right to interfere with a private organization that some fellas have set up. Some fellas and you yourself, as I understand it, Miss Starbuck. Which is one thing that makes me wonder why, having set up the committee, you're here saying bad things about it."

"I'm here—Marshal, I explained why I'm here when we arrived. I'm here to try to put a stop to Mel Bronson and others like him from taking the law into their own hands."

"We're not getting nowhere a-tall, Miss Starbuck," Collins said with an aggrieved sigh. "Why don't you just let me tend to the law, me and my deputies, and you stick to your knitting, which is cattle ranching and such like businesses."

"That's your final word on the subject, is it, Marshal?" Jessie asked as Ki rose and was about to head for the door.

"Nope, it isn't. My final word—it's a bit of advice, Miss Starbuck. Mel Bronson and other public-spirited citizens just like him are doing the people of this county a favor. You won't have any trouble with them if you keep out of trouble—keep your nose clean, as folks are fond of saying."

Jessie opened her mouth to say something more, but Ki touched her arm, distracting her. She glanced at him, and he nodded toward the door.

Once out on the street, she muttered an oath under her breath. "I can't believe what just happened in there," she said. "Marshal Collins talks about what's been done around here of late as if it were all just ever so beneficial and the men who did it were heroes worthy of public adulation."

"He sees what some of the members of the Vigilance Committee have been doing as making his job a whole lot easier, I suspect, although he never did come right out and say so in so many words. It's been my experience that lawmen like Collins are practical men. They tend to respect, if not admire, anything and everything that gets the job they're assigned to do done. The vigilantes certainly are enforcing the law in their own dangerous way, and that, I believe, makes the marshal happy."

"I've heard it said that politics makes strange bedfellows. Apparently, so does law enforcement."

"That's quite a mental picture," Ki said with a chuckle.

"What is?"

"Mel Bronson and Marshal Collins in bed together." Ki's chuckle matured into raucous laughter.

"That's not funny!"

Ki sobered. "No, I suppose it's not."

Jessie proceeded to free her horse from the hitch rail in front of the marshal's office. Ki did the same with his. Moments later, they were on their way home. But before they reached the town's western boundary, they were hailed by a rancher named Forbes who had a spread north of Jessie's.

As he rode up to them, he said, "I hear congratulations are in order, Jessie."

"Congratulations?"

"I heard about how your committee strung up Pete Damson and did away with that murderer Jerry Talbot."

"I can't take any credit for either of those events," Jessie said, her voice flat. "I wasn't present when Damson was hanged, and I tried to prevent the shooting down of Jerry Talbot."

Forbes thumbed his hat back on his head and eyed Jessie suspiciously. "I thought you were in charge of the Vigilance

97

Committee, you and Mel Bronson together."

"You've been misinformed."

"Well, anyways," Forbes said, brightening, "that bunch of yours, they don't let any grass grow under their feet, that's for sure and certain."

"What are you talking about, Mr. Forbes?" Ki asked.

"Why, I'm talking about how they've gone out hunting whoever it was stole Sid Blanton's prize stallion. It happened this morning. Sid went to see Mel Bronson about the loss of his horse. He figured the vigilantes could get it back for him if'n anybody could. Well, Bronson rounded up some of his boys and they've gone out hunting Sid's horse. God help the jasper that stole it if they should happen to find him."

"Where did they intend to look for the stallion?" Jessie asked.

"I can't tell you that. Only they know the answer to that question. But I can tell you this. If it were me that was doing the searching, I'd look in the barns of every horse breeder in the county. That stallion is worth a fortune at stud. Any man who owns him—or has him without owning him—could get him to cover a goodly number of mares and reap a handsome profit once those mares foal and the fillies and colts they drop get their growth. Yes, sirree, a handsome profit."

"We have to be on our way," Jessie told Forbes, suddenly impatient as a result of the ominous thoughts the man had aroused in her mind.

"Before you go, do you mind if I ask a question?" said Forbes.

"What's on your mind?"

"You said just now, as I recollect, that you tried to prevent the vigilantes from getting their hands on Jerry Talbot, am I right?"

"That's not exactly what I said but it's close enough, I suppose,"

"How come would you do a thing like that? Protect a cold-blooded killer, I mean, and you a vigilante your own self?"

"First of all, there's no proof that I know of that says Jerry Talbot was a killer, cold-blooded or otherwise. Secondly, although it's true I had a hand in organizing the Vigilance Committee, I am no longer a member of that committee. I hope that answers your questions, Mr. Forbes."

Jessie spurred her horse and rode down the street, Ki right behind her, leaving Forbes behind them.

"What's the hurry?" Ki asked his companion.

"I want to pay a visit to Guy Molineaux's horse ranch."

"I get it. You think that the vigilantes might suspect him of stealing Sid Blanton's stallion."

"It's a possibility. I want to warn Guy to be on the lookout for any trouble that might be riding his way in light of what we just learned from Forbes."

They rode in silence then, traveling through a land of stark vistas—barren ridges, mesas, and rocky ground. It was nearly noon by the time they reached Guy Molineaux's horse ranch, which was situated in a valley surrounded by jagged mountains. They rode down into the valley and past horses pastured in lush fields of grama grass and sweet clover on their way to the ranch house, which stood nestled among some trees on the northern perimeter of the mountain range.

Molineaux came out of the house as they rode up and waved a greeting to them. "Step down, you two, and cool your saddles," he called out cheerfully.

Jessie was delighted to see him. To see that he was hale and hearty and that the vigilantes hadn't harmed him. She silently chided herself for thinking—expecting—the worst, but then realized that she had good reason to take a morbid view of things in light of recent events involving the vigilantes.

"It's good to see you, Guy," she said as she dismounted.

"Howdy, Mr. Molineaux," Ki said as he too stepped down to the ground. "How's your breeding program going?"

"Fine and dandy, Ki, I'm pleased to be able to say. The spring increase was a good one year this year. Two strong colts and four fillies as sleek and graceful as you ever did see. It's a thrill to me every time I look at those lovely young ladies, I can tell you true."

"Has anybody else come by this way this morning?" Jessie asked.

"Why, no. It's been a quiet morning. Why do you ask, Jessie?"

"Sid Blanton had his prize stallion stolen this morning," she answered.

Before she could say any more, Molineaux frowned and said, "You don't say. Now that is a crying shame, that is. Sid must be about brokenhearted over the loss. He raised Champion from a colt. That horse had the best bloodlines of any animal within a good many miles of here. He was sired by Hollyhock Farms' Swifty out of Lucy Montague's Lady Dawn. Stolen, you say?"

"There are some men out hunting Champion," Ki told Molineaux. "Vigilantes led by Mel Bronson."

Molineaux thumbed his slouch hat back on his head. "That's bad news. You folks heard about the rampage those old boys have had of late? Oh, sorry, Jessie. I plumb forgot that you're the one that started the Vigilance Committee in the first place."

"I am coming to rue the day I did, Guy. I don't hold with their tactics. Not one whit. I thought, when we first formed the group, that we would, if we apprehended any suspected criminals, simply turn them over to the law. It hasn't worked out that way, so I've washed my hands of the whole thing insofar as participation in their manhunts and their summary executions are concerned."

"That's good news. I don't hold with vigilantism. Those kind of shenanigans can get out of hand real easy."

"We came here, Guy, when we heard about the theft of Champion," Jessie said. "We thought—"

Molineaux squinted at her. "You thought I might have stolen him to use in my own breeding program."

"No, Guy, I never for a minute thought that. I just wanted to warn you about the vigilantes being on the prowl. If they even so much as suspected you stole the horse—"

"Well, I didn't. So let them come. I'll stand up to them, you just see if I don't."

"Don't do anything foolish, Guy," Jessie warned.

Molineaux gave a hearty laugh. "I do a lot of things foolish, Jessie, and you very well know it."

"I know no such thing."

"No need to be polite about it," Molineaux declared dismissively. "You remember last spring when I got the fancy to go courting Nancy Dubois, who's all of eighteen if she's a day and me pushing fifty? That sure was foolish. I could tell you a few other foolish things I've done in the past, but I don't want to blister your ears."

"Is there anyone else around here who might take a notion to make off with Sid Blanton's stallion?" Ki asked as Molineaux laughed heartily.

"There aren't any horse thieves around here except for the occasional grub-line rider who succumbs to temptation now and then. There are those of us, though, who would dearly love to own a horse as fine as Sid's Champion. Me, for one."

Jessie felt chilled at Molineaux's admission.

"Bob Warner, for another one," he added.

"I heard Bob was going to switch from cattle to horses," Jessie said, suddenly remembering some gossip she'd heard at the barn dance she had attended the previous fall at the Grange in town. "How is he doing?"

"Not too well, I'm sorry to say. He lost two brood mares over the winter. Consumption. The best stallion he had wandered out onto the ice on Silver Lake last January, fell through, and broke his leg. Bob had to shoot him."

Jessie was silent as she weighed what Molineaux had just told her.

He continued squinting at her. "Hey, now. You're not thinking what I think you're thinking, are you?"

"I'd better ride over to Bob's place," Jessie said. "It was good seeing you again, Guy. Don't be such a stranger. Stop by the ranch when you have a chance. We'll talk. I think I can still tell taller tales than you can. Give me a chance to prove it."

"I will, Jessie. That's a promise. You tell Bob I said howdy when you see him, hear."

"I'll do that."

Molineaux waved as Jessie and Ki climbed back into their saddles and rode out.

They wheeled their horses and changed direction after leaving Molineaux. Now they headed southwest. Jessie had her horse galloping and Ki had a hard time keeping up with her. It was not until they reached Indian River that he did so. There they rode along the bank for several hundred yards until they found a good place to ford the river. They splashed into it, and their horses began to fight the strong current that was pushing them downstream. When they finally emerged from the water, they had to retrace the steps the horses had lost during the ford. But soon they were on course and heading southwest again.

Ki noticed what at first he thought were clouds gathering just above the horizon in that direction. They smeared the blue sky with their black bulk and darkened the land that lay in that direction. As he and Jessie came closer to their destination, he realized that he was seeing smoke roiling up ahead, not clouds.

Prairie fire, he thought. "Jessie."

"I see the smoke," she said before he could say anything more.

"We may be riding right into a prairie fire," he commented.

"Maybe."

They rode on. Several minutes later, they saw that there was no prairie fire to fear. There was worse. Both of them could see the flames leaping up from the burning homestead that belonged to Bob and Dolores Warner in the distance. Thick black smoke rose in billowing clouds from the building. Flames flickered like fingers in all the windows. Cinders flew through the air, setting alight the grass around the house in places before sputtering out.

"There's Dolores," Jessie said.

Dolores Warner stood in front of the house with slumped shoulders and lowered head, a woman who appeared defeated. What battle had she just fought—and lost?

Where, Ki found himself wondering, was Bob Warner, Dolores's husband? He hoped the man had not been caught inside the house when it had begun to burn. There was no sign of him anywhere in the vicinity.

He drew rein as Jessie did, and both of them quickly got out of their saddles and went over to where Dolores was still standing mute and forlorn.

She didn't look up as they approached her. She didn't speak.

"Dolores," Jessie said, reaching out tentatively to touch the woman. As her hand came to rest on Dolores Warner's shoulder, the woman flinched and looked up at her.

"Jessie?"

"Yes, dear, it's me. What happened here?"

Dolores's gaze shifted to the fire.

"What happened, Dolores?" Jessie asked a second time, speaking softly for fear of frightening the woman. She was almost sure that if she spoke in her normal tone of voice she might cause Dolores to bolt. She had seen the naked fear dancing in Dolores's eyes.

"It wasn't enough what they did," Dolores said, her voice barely audible beneath the loud crackle and snap of the flames that were devouring her home. "They had to burn the place too."

"Who did?" Jessie asked, but she thought she knew the answer to her question.

"Vigilantes."

The word hung in the air. It seemed to quiver there, a lance thrown, one that had struck and badly wounded the woman who had spoken it.

Jessie had another question, but she almost did not dare to ask it. She was saved from having to do so by Ki.

"Mrs. Warner, where's your husband?" he inquired.

Dolores looked at him. She looked at Jessie. She pointed.

At first, they thought she was pointing at the house.

"He's inside?" Jessie asked, aghast.

Dolores shook her head. She pointed again in the same direction—at the house.

Ki walked toward and then around the house. He disappeared from sight for several moments, and then reappeared.

He looked at Jessie, a grim expression on his face. She joined him. From where they stood she could see the manzanita tree that grew like a huge mushroom directly behind the house. She could also see the body of Bob Warner, his neck twisted grotesquely to one side, hanging from a rope which had been tied to one of the manzanita's lower branches.

"They killed him."

Jessie and Ki turned, startled by the sound of Dolores Warner's voice.

"They came and they killed him. Then they torched our home."

Dolores suddenly threw back her head. Staring up at the sky, her hands clenched at her sides, she let out an anguished wail. Tears streamed from her eyes and coursed down her cheeks.

Jessie, feeling an odd blend of pity and fury, put her arm around the distraught woman's thin shoulders and drew her close.

Dolores turned slightly and buried her face against Jessie's shoulder as her body was racked with sobs, the floodgate of her great grief suddenly flung wide.

Jessie held Dolores while the woman wept as if she would never stop and the waves of intense heat from the burning house swept out to engulf both the women and Ki, who stood beside them.

Finally, when Dolores's sobs had subsided into weak whimpers, Jessie held her out at arm's length and asked, "Why, Dolores? Why did they do it?"

"It was Mr. Bronson," came Dolores's ragged reply as she wiped her nose with the back of her hand. "He said Bob had stolen Sid Blanton's stallion, Champion. Bob just laughed at him. He thought Mr. Bronson was making some sort of joke. Only it wasn't a joke. As it turned out, Mr. Bronson, he was dead-shot serious. He said he didn't believe Bob. He sent some of the men with him—there were four of them and they all had guns—to search our barn back there behind the house. Well, they did what he told them to, and when they came back they were leading a stallion, and Bob, he let out a kind of gusty breath and he said, 'Where'd that animal come from?' and Mr. Bronson, he said, 'You tell us, Warner, and be quick about it.'

"Bob said the last time he'd seen that horse was in Sid Blanton's corral. Mr. Bronson said Bob had stolen it last night sometime around eight o'clock. Bob said no, he hadn't done no such thing. He said he was over to Mike Anderson's place from seven to nine last night. Mr. Bronson, he said, 'Possession is nine tenths of the law,' whatever that means, and then he gave the men siding him an order and they grabbed ahold of Bob and they dragged him back behind the house.

"I ran after them, trying to tear Bob free, but those men had ahold of him like they weren't ever going to let loose of him. I cried, I remember, but it didn't soften their hearts one little bit. Somebody came up with a rope, and it was then I realized what they were fixing to do to my Bob. I fought them, Jessie. I fought them as hard as ever I could, but it didn't help Bob. I was too weak. Besides which, they were four and I but one going up against all of them.

"They—one of them, it was Junior Dell—held me tight with my arms pinned behind me, and I had to stand there and watch while they strung my man up on that tree back there behind the house. I kept yelling at them. I told them that Bob was over at the Anderson place at the time they said that horse was stolen so he couldn't have done it. 'Oh, let him be!' I said. 'Please, you all, let my man *be*!' "

Dolores started to sag. Jessie reached out to support her.

"They paid me no mind, Jessie. They just did what they came to do, and pretty soon, when Junior Dell kicked the stool out from under Bob, he swung. They'd no sooner done that than they went and set fire to the house. Mr. Bronson, he said something like let this be a lesson to any horse thief who happens to hear about it. Then they rode out with Mr. Bronson leading Mr. Blanton's stallion that had somehow or other got itself into our barn."

"What are you going to do now, Dolores?" Jessie asked. "Is there someplace you can stay?"

105

Dolores looked around her as if she had never seen the area before. "They left the barn standing," she said. "I'll stay in there if the weather turns nasty. I can sleep in the hayloft. I've got to cut Bob down. I've got to bury my man. Oh, it's a terrible thing that's happened to us, Jessie. I always had a secret hope. I always hoped I'd be the one to go first. I didn't want to stay on in a world where Bob wasn't. Whatever will I do now with him gone and me so heart-hurt I don't even care if the sun rises tomorrow?"

Jessie knew there was nothing she could say, nothing that could offer even the smallest kind of comfort.

"I've got to bury Bob," Dolores said numbly. "I'll ride over to Miz Bettincourt's. Maybe she'll lend me a hand."

"I'm sure she will," Jessie said. "I'll go with you."

"Would you, Jessie? I'd be much obliged to you if you would. I don't like to sound like a weak sister, but I've got to say I feel like those vigilantes have went and pulled the rug right out from under me and I'm not one bit sure of my footing anymore."

"Ki, I'll see you at home later on," Jessie said.

He nodded, and stood watching as Jessie accompanied Dolores to the barn. He waited until they reemerged some time later with Jessie driving a fringe-topped surrey to which she had tied her horse, Dolores seated beside her.

He watched them drive away, and then he went back to his horse, stepped into the saddle, and headed home, thinking that burying the dead was getting to be a more common than normal event in the community of late, thanks in large part to the lethal actions of the vigilantes.

" 'Jesus said unto her, I am the resurrection, and the life: he that believeth in me, though he were dead, yet shall he live . . . ' "

The words of the preacher sounded sonorous on the soft air as Jessie stood with Ki beside the gaping grave the following afternoon and Dolores Warner wept openly over the closed pine coffin that contained the body of her late husband.

" 'And whosoever liveth and believeth in me shall never die.' "

Jessie stood and listened to the words of the preacher, with her hands demurely folded but her mind racing as she thought of what had been done to Bob Warner and by whom. Beside her, Ki stood with head bowed. He was wearing his best three-piece suit, which she had pressed for him before they left for what would be the first of two funerals to be held that afternoon. Jerry Talbot was to be buried an hour from now.

" . . . and we pray that the good God in His lofty heaven above," the minister was saying as he closed his worn bible, "will give our sister, Dolores, the strength to endure the woe that has settled on her shoulders. We pray that He, in his infinite wisdom and boundless mercy, will show her the light of His everlasting love and make her know and understand that our beloved brother, Robert, is not dead but alive and residing today in a better place where he will live forever. . . ."

There was more, but Jessie hardly heard the earnest words of the minister as an image of Mel Bronson's face materialized before her and she saw him smug in his self-righteousness. She found herself despising the man. Hating him and what he had done. She glanced covertly at the minister as if he might have been able to divine her uncharitable thoughts. But he seemed oblivious to all save the sound of his own mellifluous voice. She found herself paying more attention to Dolores Warner's heartbroken sobs than she was to what he was saying.

Soon, it was almost over. The pallbearers lowered the coffin into the ground. Dolores stepped to the side of the hole in the ground, where she stooped and picked up a handful of dirt, which she tossed down upon the pine box. The minister gave a final benediction, and then the mourners began to move away from the hole in the ground that spoke dumbly of death, and off into that other world, that more familiar and much more comfortable one, where they would soon speak to one another of such mundane things as the threat of rain and the rapidly rising cost of coffee.

Ki took Jessie's arm. Together they went over to where Dolores was standing and accepting condolences from the

107

people who had attended the funeral.

When it was her turn, Jessie embraced Dolores and then whispered words she knew could give the bereaved woman little more than cold comfort. She stepped aside, and Ki shook hands with Dolores and said similar words. Then they both turned and went to where their buggy awaited them.

"This," Ki said, as they climbed into the buggy and he picked up the reins, "is a day of death."

"This," Jessie said, "seems to be a season of death, not just a day."

They drove in silence to the Talbot ranch. When they arrived, they found a cluster of black-garbed men and women already there. Bud Talbot stood with the minister in the well-tended patch of grassy ground behind the house that served as the Talbot family's burial ground.

Ki parked the buggy and then walked with Jessie to the graveside, where they waited in strained silence for the second funeral of the day to begin. Jessie, glancing covertly at Bud, thought he had earlier given her a look of . . . Of what? Contempt? Anger? She wasn't sure. There was something in the firm set of his jaw and in the way his eyes met hers that chilled her.

"Dearly beloved," said the minister, "we are gathered here today to bid farewell to . . ."

The familiar ritual proceeded apace. When at last it was over and most of the people had driven away, Jessie and Ki made their way over to Bud to offer him their condolences.

He turned his back on them.

They exchanged uneasy glances.

Then Jessie said, "We're sorry—"

Bud spun around to face her. "You're sorry, are you? It's partly your fault that my brother is in that hole we dug today. You helped put him there. If it hadn't been for you and others of your ilk who went and formed that damned Vigilance Committee, Jerry would be alive today."

"Bud, that's not fair," a shocked Jessie protested.

"Nor is it true," Ki declared.

"Get out!" Bud barked. "You're not welcome here, Jessie. So get out and don't come back!"

His words were like a whip striking her. Jessie recoiled from them. She wanted to turn and run, to flee from their lacerating blows. She tried once more to speak to Bud, but he strode away from her.

"He'll come around," the minister told her. "He's very upset. Forgive him."

Jessie turned and, with Ki walking by her side, made her way back to the buggy. All the way home, she fought back the tears that told not only of her sorrow at Jerry Talbot's untimely death but also of that other death that was equally devastating—the death of the long-time friendship that had existed between her and Bud Talbot.

★

Chapter 7

Jessie awoke before dawn the next morning after a restless night of tossing and turning, bad dreams and troubled thoughts.

Sid Blanton. Champion. Dolores Warner. Bob Warner.

The names echoed and reechoed in her mind. She gazed out through the window at the new moon drifting so serenely in the sky as if to mock her own anxieties that had kept her from sleeping most of the night.

Bob Warner was dead because he had been accused of stealing the horse named Champion from Sid Blanton. Champion had been found, to Bob Warner's surprise according to his wife, in the Warner barn. Dolores Warner had said that her husband couldn't have stolen the horse because he had been at Mike Anderson's place at the time the horse was stolen.

Jessie turned over on her left side, tucked her hands under her pillow, and tried to go to sleep. After twenty more minutes of fruitlessly courting sleep that would not come to her, she threw off the sheet covering her and got up. She washed, using the porcelain basin and china pitcher

111

full of water that sat on her dresser. As she dressed, the first light of false dawn streaked the black sky, turning the part of it nearest the horizon gray.

Once dressed, she made her way downstairs and into the kitchen. Yawning, she made herself a pot of coffee, dropping a few eggshells she had saved for the purpose into the pot to settle the grounds. When it was boiling, she poured herself a cup and sat down at the table to drink it black.

As tension stirred by her thoughts rose within her, she got to her feet and, carrying her cup of coffee, began to pace the room. She circled the table, and then circled it again. If she could prove that Bob Warner was nowhere near Sid Blanton's place at the time Blanton's horse, Champion, had been stolen, she could return to Marshal Collins and tell the lawman what she had found out. Surely, then, Collins would have to take action against Mel Bronson and the other members of the Vigilance Committee to stop the bloodshed and hangings they had been responsible for.

She knew Mike Anderson. He and his wife, Betsy, were old friends. She made up her mind to go and talk to him. If he would state that Bob Warner was with him at the time Champion was stolen, she was sure she could make a case strong enough to force Marshal Collins to take action against the vigilantes. Collins would have no choice but to do so if she could prove that the vigilantes, led by Bronson, had lynched an innocent man.

As excitement, hope, and impatience all stirred within her, a heady blend of emotions, she decided to go at once to speak to Anderson instead of waiting, as she had at first planned to do, for Ki to get up. She drank the last of her coffee, washed the cup, and then went out to the barn, where she saddled and bridled her mare. She led the horse out of the barn into the light of the sun, which was an incomplete orange globe as it began to rise above the eastern horizon. She swung into the saddle, wheeled her mount, and rode out.

The mare stepped high and tossed its head. It fought the bit, forcing Jessie to keep it under tight rein. Its early morning vigor, which bordered on skittishness, matched Jessie's own sense of jumpiness. The pair tore across the prairie, Jessie's unbound coppery hair flying out behind her as the mare galloped along as if it were in a race for its life.

Less than an hour later, they arrived at Mike Anderson's place. Jessie and the mare, both of them still keyed up, jumped the snake-pole fence that surrounded the Anderson's homeplace. She drew rein in front of the sod house and dismounted. She was about to knock on the door when she hesitated. She looked up. The sun was above the horizon— but just barely. She hoped Mike and Betsy Anderson and their young daughter, Eva, were early risers.

Betsy responded to her knock and, when she saw who her visitor was, she gave a little yelp of delight. "Jessie Starbuck, you are surely a sight for sore eyes! We haven't seen you in far too long a time. Where do you keep yourself and what brings you here at this early hour?"

"Betsy, I've been remiss in my neighborly duties. I've been meaning to come to call on you and Mike for ever so long, but something always seemed to pop up and keep me from doing so. I trust you will forgive my bad manners."

"You're here now. That's what counts, isn't it? Come in. Have you had breakfast?"

"No. A cup of coffee but no breakfast."

"Then come in and sit down at the table. You'll take breakfast with Mike and me. Eva's still asleep, thank goodness. Once she's up—Jessie, I tell you that four-year-old is a caution. She keeps me on the go all day long, that child does."

Jessie followed Betsy into the house, closing the door behind her, and took the chair Betsy pulled out for her. "Where's Mike?"

"He went out to the chicken coop to gather the eggs. I'll go call him."

Betsy went to the door, opened it, and called out, "Mike, we've got company. Come on in."

Several minutes later, as Betsy was setting a plate of grits and fried pork rinds in front of Jessie, Mike Anderson came into the house and stopped when he saw his guest, the expression on his face somber.

"You look like your favorite dog just died," Betsy playfully chided him when she saw his expression. "Aren't you glad to see Jessie?"

"Hello, Mike," Jessie said as Betsy placed a cup brimming with coffee by her plate.

"You come about Vigilante Committee business, have you?" he asked, setting the wicker basket full of eggs he was carrying on the table and then sitting down opposite Jessie.

"In a way, yes, I did."

"Well, I'm in no mood to talk to any vigilante."

"Mike!" a shocked Betsy exclaimed. "That's no way to talk to an old friend."

"It's the way to talk to a vigilante, and she's one of them."

"He's upset, Jessie," Betsy hurriedly explained, pouring oil on obviously troubled waters. "We heard about what happened to Bob Warner."

"Mike," Jessie said, "I'm not associated with the Vigilance Committee any longer."

He studied her, his eyes hostile, a muscle in his jaw jumping. "You said you come here about vigilante business."

"In a way, I have. But not as a member of the committee. I was told by Dolores Warner that Bob Warner was here at the time Sid Blanton claims his stallion was stolen. Is that a fact?"

"It is. But as far as the time goes, I don't know what time it was when he came by. Our wall clock's on the blink and I had to pawn my Waltham watch a month ago to buy a new plow. I know it was dark is all."

"Would you say it was around eight o'clock?"

"Could have been. Can't say for sure."

"It must have been," Betsy volunteered. "We had put Eva to bed about an hour before Bob arrived—right after sundown. So it must have been around eight o'clock."

"Is that when Blanton's horse was took?" Mike asked.

"So I've been told. Was Bob here very long?"

"Not long. He brought back an ax he'd borrowed from me."

Jessie spooned grits into her mouth. Then, after swallowing, she asked, "How long would you say he was here?"

"I already told you he wasn't here long a-tall. He come and he set for a spell and then he left."

Jessie had the distinct impression that Mike Anderson was not particularly interested in talking to her or answering her questions. She noticed that he avoided looking directly at her when he did speak.

"We heard the Vigilance Committee hanged him," Betsy said in a voice softer than her usually hearty one. "That was a terrible thing. My heart goes out to poor Dolores. Whatever will she do now without her man?"

"Out here in the West," Mike said, "stealing a man's horse is still a capital crime in a lot of places."

Jessie looked at him in surprise. She put down the coffee cup she had been about to drink from and said, "As far as I know, there's no proof of any kind that Bob Warner stole Sid Blanton's stallion."

"Folks are saying the vigilantes found it in his barn," Mike said, getting up and pouring himself a cup of coffee. "If that's not proof, I reckon I don't know what is."

"The fact that Champion was found in his barn," Jessie said somewhat testily, "doesn't prove that Bob stole the horse and put it there."

Anderson gave her a covert glance, but said nothing more.

"Jessie, I know the Warners were friends of yours the same as we are," Betsy began tentatively. "But you've got to admit that it looks bad about Bob. The horse was in his barn and not in Mr. Blanton's, where it belonged."

"What's your interest in all this?" Anderson asked Jessie.

"I think Bob Warner might have been innocent of the charge the vigilantes leveled against him."

"You don't think he made off with Mr. Blanton's horse?" a wide-eyed Betsy asked.

"I don't know, to tell you the truth," Jessie replied. "But I think the vigilantes acted hastily, to put it mildly. A better word might be precipitously. You know they shot

Jerry Talbot down in cold blood because they claimed he killed a man."

"Killed a man," Anderson said pointedly, "who he told the world he meant to kill."

Jessie felt like a swimmer swimming against the tide. Anderson seemed determined to counter everything she said. Did he believe both men were guilty? She asked him if he did.

"It would appear so," was his blunt answer.

"But Bob Warner had an alibi for the time the stallion was stolen," Jessie pointed out, the remaining food on her plate forgotten.

"Says who?" Anderson asked.

"*You* can say so if you just will."

"All I know is Bob Warner come by here and then he went away again real quick. Maybe he had horse-thieving on his mind. Maybe that's why he didn't linger the other night."

"Look, Mike," Jessie said, "I came here to ask you a favor. I came to ask you to go with me to Marshal Collins and tell him that Bob Warner was here the night Champion disappeared around eight o'clock."

"I never said no such a thing. I told you I didn't know what time Warner was here on account of my clock was broken and I had no watch."

"But you could at least tell the marshal that he was here and that it was dark when he arrived. Betsy, you could come with us. You could tell the marshal the same thing."

"Oh, no, Jessie, I couldn't do that."

Jessie stared at Betsy in amazement. "You couldn't? Why couldn't you?"

"Jessie," Mike said, "these vigilantes that Mel Bronson's got scouring the countryside for all kinds of evil men, they're a force to reckon with. Bob Warner found that out, to his everlasting sorrow. So did Jerry Talbot and some rustlers and I don't know how many other unlucky fellows. I'm not going up against them, and neither is Betsy. We're law-abiding folks and we don't want to call attention to ourselves."

"Bob's right," Betsy said. "There's little Eva to think of. What would become of the child if something happened to us?"

At last Jessie understood. "You're telling me that you're both afraid to go to the law about what happened to Bob Warner. You could at least salvage his reputation posthumously if you did—if you provided him with an alibi for the night of the theft."

"There's nothing we can do," Betsy said. "We can't bring Bob back from the dead."

"Let the dead bury the dead," her husband declared dolefully. "The living have to look after themselves."

"The vigilantes wouldn't harm you if you went to the law with me," Jessie said. "Telling the law what you know is no crime."

"You can't say that with any kind of certainty, Jessie," Anderson said. "They can do anything they damn well please, and you know that as well as I do."

"But if you were to go to Marshal Collins," Jessie argued, "and tell him that Bob Warner was here at the time the Blanton horse was stolen, you might be able to prevent other hangings of innocent men. The vigilantes would be discredited on the basis of your testimony."

"Mike, maybe Jessie's right," Betsy suggested uncertainly. "Maybe we should—"

"What we should do is let sleeping dogs lie," Mike thundered, slamming a fist down onto the table to rattle the dishes resting on it.

Jessie rose and bade good-bye to the Andersons. She left the house, and moments later she was riding away, her failure to convince them to provide a legitimate alibi for Bob Warner rankling within her.

When she got home, she found Ki up and waiting for her.

"You had a visitor while you were gone," he informed her.

"I did? Who was it?"

"Moses Slater."

"Oh, I'm sorry I missed him. I haven't seen Moses in a while. What did he want, did he say?"

"Well, he wasn't specific, but I gather it had something to do with what's been happening around here lately."

"You mean the vigilantes' activities?"

"That's the impression I got, although he didn't come right out and say so in so many words. He did say, as I recall, that what he had to tell you was important and would 'curl your hair and stand you straight up on your toes.' "

"I wonder what it could be."

"At the moment, that's his deep dark secret. He asked me when you'd be back, and I told him I didn't have any idea since you'd left this morning before I'd gotten up and I didn't know where you had gone. Where did you go, by the way?"

"I paid a call on the Andersons. I wanted them to go with me into town and tell their stories to Marshal Collins."

"Their stories?"

"About Bob Warner having been at their place at the approximate time that Sid Blanton's stallion was stolen."

"Did they? Go into town with you?"

Jessie shook her head. "They refused to. Ki, they were scared. Scared of Bronson and his vigilantes. They—Mike especially—took the position that they didn't want to make trouble, and they feared that if they told what they knew to the marshal, they would be making trouble for the vigilantes and that, in turn, might make trouble for them."

Ki whistled through his teeth. "It seems the vigilantes have put a scare into the righteous as well as the wicked around here."

"It would appear so," Jessie said, unable to keep the disgust she was feeling from coloring her tone. "That is not a healthy situation. In fact, I think it's a dangerous situation. The mere fact that good law-abiding people like the Andersons have come to feel that they dare not do anything to cross the vigilantes for fear of reprisals automatically grants more power to the vigilantes. Power they would not ordinarily, and under normal conditions, have."

"You're suggesting that the vigilantes and their leader, Mel Bronson, are corrupt as a result of the power they have at the present time?"

"Not necessarily. The thought just crossed my mind, that's all. I think maybe I should ride over to Moses's place and see what it was he wanted to see me about."

"There's no real need to do that. When I told him that I didn't know exactly when you'd be back, he said he'd stop by again tomorrow. He was on his way to town, he said, to do some shopping."

"I'm looking forward to seeing him. He was my childhood hero, you know."

"No, I didn't."

"Oh, my, yes. Moses was in his early thirties when I was a young girl. He used to work for my father at that time here on the ranch as a bronc-buster. To me, he was something very very special. I confess I thought he was just about the handsomest man I'd ever seen. He had blue eyes that could bore holes in iron and broad shoulders and strong hands, the like of which I'd never seen on a man before. He was soft-spoken, and he knew well the trail that led to a young girl's heart.

"If I did something wrong, Moses was the first one to speak up in my defense. My father would be ready to go for the switch sometimes, but Moses would step in and, in that sweet-talking way of his, persuade my father that I had done no wrong. Or very little, at any rate."

"He sounds like every young girl's dream. A knight in brightly shining armor."

"Oh, he was all of that and more." Jessie closed her eyes for a moment, fondly remembering her long-ago relationship with Moses Slater. Then opening her eyes and smiling, she told Ki, "We had a secret, Moses and I. It was a hiding place of sorts. You know that old pine tree down by Big Bend?"

"The one that stands like a green sentinel at the crossroads there?"

"That's the one. I'll bet you didn't know that it has a secret hiding place in its trunk down near the ground. One that's almost impossible to see if you didn't know it was there."

"No, I didn't."

"Neither did anyone else. Except Moses Slater. He told me about it one day. He told me the fairies used it to send messages to one another. Well, at the time he told me that, I considered myself quite the grown-up young lady and I told him most emphatically that I didn't believe in fairies.

"He said that was my right and he didn't blame me one bit for being a disbeliever. But he said it might behoove me, were I ever in the vicinity of Big Bend, to look for the fairies' secret hiding place and see what I just might find in it.

"I told him I was far too busy to indulge in such foolishness. But the minute he rode off I made a beeline for Big Bend. I found the hole in the tree trunk and I also found a note—one that might have been written by a spider—or a fairy—it was so delicately inscribed."

"A note? What did it say?"

"It said—I shall never forget what it said. It said:

> Roses are red
> Violets are blue
> Sugar is sweet
> And Jessie Starbuck is too

"I was overwhelmed to think that the fairies even knew about me, let alone that they thought I was sweet. I ran straight to Moses with the note, and he read it and said the fairies knew exactly what they were talking about and that they never made a mistake about such things. Imagine that! To find a secret message from the fairies that mentioned me and to hear the man I absolutely idolized say he thought I was sweet—all in the same otherwise ordinary day!"

"Where are you off to?" Ki asked Jessie two days later when he arrived home from a visit to town and found her getting ready to go out.

"I thought I'd take a ride over to Moses Slater's place."

"Then he never did show up like he said he would?"

"No, he didn't. And I find that strange. Moses was always a man of his word. He would have shown up if he could."

"The way you put it—it sounds ominous. Are you suggesting you think something's happened to him?"

"I don't know. I just think I should go to his place and see if there is anything wrong. After all, he told you what he had to talk to me about was important. So why didn't he return to see me as he told you he would?"

"Maybe he decided that what he thought was so important wasn't all that important after all."

"I'll see you later, Ki."

Jessie left the house and went to the barn, where she got her horse ready to ride and then rode out, heading for the Slater homestead.

When she arrived at it, she knew at once that something was wrong.

Her hand went to her jacket pocket, where her double-barreled derringer rested. She looked around, but saw no one and heard nothing. The silence was oppressive and weighed heavily on her. Drawing her gun, she carefully dismounted and walked slowly toward the house.

"Moses!" she called out when she was a few feet away from the broken door.

No reply.

She called again, and again received no answer. She went up to the door, her gun leveled, and peered into the dim interior of the house. The place was a shambles. Tables and chairs were overturned. Crockery that should have been safely shelved in cupboards lay smashed on the floor. Drawers were open and their contents strewn about on the floor. The mattress on the rope bed had been slashed, and so had the pillow, and straw from both of them had been strewn all over the floor. Even cans of coffee and flour and sugar had been opened and dumped.

Vandals?

She wasn't sure. She finally decided that the scene looked more as if someone had been searching for something. If so, she was sure she knew what they were searching for.

They? Who?

She left the house and went to the outhouse, which stood on a rise behind it. Moses Slater was not inside the building. Nor was he in his barn. His horse was also missing.

Jessie began to walk around the area, studying the ground as she went. She found a few prints left by boots with underslung heels on the hardpan surrounding the homestead. She also found prints that had been made by bare feet. In one place, not far from the barn, she saw signs of a struggle and the prints of a single horse's hooves. It had headed for the woods in the distance.

She found a trail left by booted feet that also led into the woods, and followed it to a spot where some horses had been tied. They had left evidence of their presence there in the nibbled bark of some young yellow pines.

Moses Slater, she decided, had been taken by persons unknown who had broken into his house. But the way she read the sign surrounding the house, Moses had escaped from his attackers and fled barefoot to the barn, where he'd boarded his horse and ridden out. Whoever had broken down the door of his house and apparently ransacked it had ridden out in pursuit of him.

She went back to her horse and climbed into the saddle. Then she rode out following the now-cold trail left by the men she was convinced had gone out after Moses when he escaped from them.

Fear traveled with her as she rode through a stark treeless landscape. Images of Jerry Talbot lying bloody and lifeless on the ground and of Bob Warner's hanged body swaying in the wind raced through her mind, turning her skin clammy and her mouth dry.

She walked her horse as she scanned the arid ground. She lost the trail at one point, and spent nearly a half hour searching for it again. She finally found it some distance away beyond the stretch of stony ground that made the trailing difficult.

Soon she arrived at a spot near Big Bend where the riders chasing Moses had paused, apparently to reconnoiter the area. She had lost track of Moses's sign, which had been covered up by those who were pursuing him. Apparently at this point they had also lost track of him.

One rider had headed east. Another west. The others had remained where they were. Jessie scouted the area, and soon found signs that told her that the rider who had headed east in the direction of the crossroads, near Big Bend had returned and that someone else had been riding with him.

Moses Slater? She supposed so because, when those two riders had joined the others who had remained in place, the entire group had moved out. They had stopped when they reached the first tree they had come to that was tall enough to hang a man from.

Jessie drew rein and stared at the body hanging from the tree directly in front of her. The body of Moses Slater. His hands were tied behind his back. He wore no shoes, only a pair of trousers. His upper body was bare. There was no sign of his horse.

She sat her saddle, her hands wrapped tightly around her saddlehorn as if she were trying to prevent herself from falling to the ground, and felt the tears well up, then spill out of her eyes and roll down her cheeks as she stared at the remains of her friend.

Uncounted and unnoticed minutes passed as she sat there staring, unable to take her eyes away from the terrible sight confronting her. The lifeless body, silent though it was, told her the story of what she believed had happened. She was sure of it now. The fact that Moses wore no shoes or shirt suggested to her that he had been attacked while in bed. But he had managed to escape from his attackers and ride out. One of them had caught up with him at Big Bend and brought him back. Then all of them had ridden on until they found a hanging tree.

Jessie was sure she knew who had done this. Vigilantes. What she did not know was why they had done it. Two thoughts were uppermost in her mind. She wanted—and vowed she would get—vengeance. Not only for Moses Slater but also for Jerry Talbot, and even for Pritchard and the other two rustlers who had stolen her stock, and the others who had been summarily executed by Mel Bronson and the vigilantes under his control. None of those men deserved to die, she passionately believed, the way they all did—without a chance to defend themselves in a court of law.

The second thought that roiled in Jessie's mind was why Moses had met his death in such an ugly fashion. What possible crime could he have committed that would have set the vigilantes on his trail? She intended to find out.

She forced herself to walk her horse away from the silent tableau of death. There was nothing she could do at the moment for Moses Slater. She didn't even have a knife with which to cut him down.

She forced herself to sit up straight in the saddle, and then she lashed her horse into a fast gallop.

By the time she reached town, she was sweaty and her stomach felt sour. She paid no attention to either condition as she left her horse hitched to the rail in front of Marshal Collins's office and went inside.

Collins was there, seated behind his desk, and he looked up at Jessie with an expression of what appeared to her to be distaste on his face. She ignored it.

"Moses Slater is dead," she announced without greeting or any other kind of preamble. "His body's hanging from a tree just west of Big Bend."

"So I've been told," Collins said matter-of-factly.

"You knew about the hanging?"

"I just found out about it a little while ago. My deputy, Whit Price, heard the talk that's making the rounds in town."

"What talk?"

"The vigilantes decided to do old Mose in."

So I was right, Jessie thought, but she said nothing, waiting for Collins to continue.

"It seems that Moses was in town the other day. They say he spent some time drinking in the Last Chance Saloon. I guess the whiskey he consumed there must have overheated his blood. On his way out of town, his eye got caught by Miss Evelyn Pruitt. He must have followed her home. It was there that he raped her."

Collins's words stunned Jessie. For a moment, she couldn't speak.

"Old Mose, it would seem, had turned hard and horny in his old age," Colling commented with a snicker, watching Jessie to see if he had managed to shock her.

"How do you know all this—about the—about what happened to Evelyn Pruitt?" Jessie asked him.

"I already told you that. Whit Price, my deputy, told me. Everybody in town's talking about it, Whit says. They're saying old Mose got what he deserved and they're glad, by and large, that Miss Pruitt had the good sense to go to Mel Bronson and report what had happened to her at the hands of that old goat Moses."

"Why didn't she come to you?" Jessie asked. "After all, you're the law around here—supposedly."

The sarcasm implicit in her last word was not lost on Collins. He glared at Jessie. "I don't know why Miss Pruitt saw fit to go to Mel Bronson instead of coming here to me. But I can guess. The Vigilance Committee has been doing a pretty good job of rousting out the criminals who've been preying on people around here of late. So I guess she figured they could help her get even with old Mose for what he went and did to her. If that is what she thought, well, she was right. The vigilantes rode right out and—well, you know the end of the story."

"Marshal, I have to say I think what has been going on around here lately is absolutely unconscionable. I think you should do something about it instead of sitting by and just letting matters take their course. A course, I submit to you, that is a dangerous one. I refer to the fact that another man is dead, and I wonder if anyone ever thought to question Miss Pruitt concerning the charge she made against Moses Slater."

"Question her?"

"Yes, question her. Maybe she wasn't telling the truth. Maybe—maybe she lured Moses to her home. Maybe she was the one who initiated the encounter she claims occurred. It's even possible that nothing at all happened."

"Miss Starbuck, you can't be serious! If nothing at all happened, why would a decent and upright woman like Evelyn Pruitt make such a serious charge against old Mose?"

Jessie searched for a reasonable answer to Collins's question. She came up with, "Maybe the woman had a grudge of some kind against Moses. Maybe this was her way of getting even with him."

"You think Moses was innocent, do you?"

"I do."

"You've got no proof that he is—was."

"And you and your precious vigilantes have no real proof that Moses was *guilty*!"

Collins shrugged.

"You ought to arrest those vigilantes for murder," Jessie cried, her temper lost. "By the way, did anybody tell your deputy that they ransacked Moses's house?"

"No."

"Well, they did. The place was a mess, a complete mess. Now why do you suppose the vigilantes did that?"

"I have no idea—if it really was done and they did it."

"Oh, it was done, all right. I was there and saw what had been done. I also happen to have an idea why it was done. Did you ever hear Moses tell the story of the one big love affair of his life?"

"Can't say as I have."

"Well, suffice it to say that he bought a girl a diamond ring a long time ago, and then, when the romance ended, she returned the ring and he kept it as kind of sad souvenir of his lost love. I believe the vigilantes ransacked his house in an effort to find and steal that diamond."

"You don't know that for a fact."

"Don't I? Give me one other good reason why they ransacked Moses's house."

"You don't even know they did ransack it. Maybe it was somebody come by after they'd taken old Mose away with them."

Jessie had to admit to herself that what Collins had just said could very well be true. She realized she was behaving in the same way as the vigilantes she had been condemning.

126

Making judgments without adequate proof to support them. The fact that the vigilantes had taken Moses, she realized, did not necessarily mean they were the ones who had ransacked his house. That could have been done at a later time and by someone other than the vigilantes.

"You ask me, you're beginning to sound a whole lot like the pot calling the kettle black," Collins said with a smirk.

"There's another thing I want to mention to you as long as I'm here," Jessie persisted. "I learned from Dolores Warner that her husband, Bob, had been visiting Mike and Betsy Anderson at the time Sid Blanton's stallion, Champion, was stolen. But Bob Warner was nevertheless hanged by the vigilantes because they found Champion in the Warner barn when they came by there. They claimed that the presence of the horse in the barn was sufficient proof that Bob Warner had stolen it. They wouldn't listen to the Warners' claim that Bob was at the Andersons at the time the horse was taken."

"Miss Starbuck, I'm a very busy man. Why don't you stop beating about the bush and get right down to the point. That would save us both some time, if you were to do that."

"I wasn't beating about the bush, as you put it, Marshal. I was telling you something I think is very important. But the basic point is this. Bob Warner may well have been innocent. I think if you had done your duty you would have found out on your own what I just told you."

"What do you want me to do about it now?" Collins asked, ignoring Jessie's criticism.

"You could go and talk to the Andersons."

"About Bob Warner's supposed alibi."

"About Bob Warner's alibi," Jessie amended pointedly.

"I already told you I'm a busy man. If the Andersons have something they want to say to me, they're welcome to come in here to the office and speak their piece. I'll listen. It's one of the things I'm paid to do."

"What you're paid to do, Marshal," Jessie said angrily, "you do not, in my humble opinion, do very well at all. So I'll tell you this. I'm perfectly capable of taking up the

127

slack you leave behind in doing your duty. I'm going to find a way to put a stop to the killings, Marshal. I don't know at the moment just how I'm going to do that, I confess, but I assure you wholeheartedly that I am going to do it. I feel partially responsible for what's been going on. I was one of the people who sincerely believed that the formation of a Vigilance Committee would be good for our community."

"You don't think it's been good? The way it's been clearing out the criminals from around here?"

"Not when the tactics it uses flout the law, no, I don't think so."

"You're saying the vigilantes—all of them respectable men, I'd like to point out—are lawbreakers. I say they're more like ministers of justice, that's what I say."

"Obviously we do not see eye to eye on the matter, Marshal."

"One thing before you go, Miss Starbuck," Collins said as Jessie opened the door. "Don't you go and do anything foolish. In fact, it might be a whole lot better if you didn't do anything at all where the Vigilance Committee is concerned. They're powerful men and their committee's a powerful force that I, for one, wouldn't want to lock horns with. Maybe you shouldn't either."

Jessie stared incredulously at Collins. "Are you saying the vigilantes—men like Mel Bronson, some of whom I've known most of my life—would dare to try to do me harm for trying to put a stop to their lawless acts of bloody vengeance?"

"Don't go putting words in my mouth," Collins snapped. "What I said—call it good advice."

Jessie grimaced. "I understand now, Marshal. You're afraid to stand up to Bronson and the others. That's it, isn't it?"

"I'm not known as a fear-filled man. I've been in any number of shootouts—"

"You're a coward, Marshal, that's what you are."

Collins shot to his feet. Leaning over his desk and shaking an index finger at Jessie, he barked, "That's enough out of you! I won't tolerate such talk from you or anybody else.

128

You'd better be on your merry way, Miss Starbuck. You're not welcome here."

Jessie turned on her heels and left the office.

"You'd best watch your step!" Collins shouted after her. "You might think it's smart to start stepping on some important toes in this town, but it could turn out to be the dumbest thing you ever did. People whose toes get stepped on often as not get even with the one as did the stepping in the first place."

★

Chapter 8

Jessie left the coroner's office, which she had visited to arrange for the retrieval and burial of the body of Moses Slater following her departure from Marshal Collins's office.

Her next stop was to be made at the home of Evelyn Pruitt. It took her no more than five minutes to arrive at the clap-board house that was painted a bright white and situated on a street made shady by tall elms lining both sides of it. She went through the gate in the white picket fence and up to the front door.

It was opened almost immediately in response to her knock by Vincent Pruitt, Evelyn's father, a middle-aged man with thick jowls and muttonchop gray whiskers.

"Good day, Vincent," Jessie greeted him. "I've come to see Evelyn. Is she at home?"

"I take it you've heard what happened, Jessica," Pruitt said mournfully.

"Yes, I've heard. It was news I wish I hadn't had to hear."

"Come in, come in."

Jessie stepped into the foyer and then, when Pruitt had closed the door, followed him into a parlor filled with heavy claw-footed furniture. She took a seat in an upholstered wing chair into which Pruitt waved her before sitting down opposite her.

"I'm afraid Evelyn is indisposed," he intoned, steepling his fingers and sighing softly. "As you might imagine, her recent ordeal has quite severely upset her."

"I can understand that," Jessie said, trying not to let her disappointment show on her face. "When do you think I might call and talk with her, Vincent?"

"Soon, I expect. Tomorrow perhaps. Evelyn is young and the young, no matter how mightily they may suffer, have resilience and tend to recover from their injuries, whether physical or mental, rather rapidly."

Pruitt paused, patting the tips of his steepled fingers together. "I'm sure Evelyn will be pleased to learn that you came to call and offer her your sympathy for all she has suffered."

"I didn't come just to offer her my sympathy, Vincent."

"Oh?" Raised eyebrows. "What else did you come calling for, Jessica, if I may inquire?"

"I wanted to ask her to tell me exactly what happened."

"Evelyn would rather not talk about the horror, and I must say I'm surprised that you want to force her to."

"Are you aware, Vincent, that the vigilantes, led by Mel Bronson, hanged Moses Slater for his alleged crime against your daughter?"

"Yes, I am fully aware of that."

"Quite frankly, I have great difficulty in believing that Moses could have done what he is said to have done. I thought Evelyn might be able to convince me that it really did happen."

"You doubt my daughter's veracity?"

Avoiding answering Pruitt's question, Jessie said, "I'll drop by again tomorrow, Vincent. Perhaps by then Evelyn will feel strong enough to talk to me."

"Evelyn would not lie about such a thing," Pruitt insisted.

"Is there a chance, do you think, that she could have been mistaken about what happened? I mean she might have misinterpeted Moses's attentions to her as something other than what they really were. They might actually have been quite innocent—"

"Nonsense! The man attacked Evelyn. I'm glad the Vigilance Committee did what they did. Glad, I tell you, that that beast Slater is dead and will never again have an opportunity to harm an innocent girl like my daughter."

"You know of course, Vincent, that there have been other hangings carried out by the vigilantes in recent days."

"Yes, I know. The vigilantes have been both alert and active, for which I, for one, am most grateful. I never did think I would stand in need of their services, but when the need did arise, Mel Bronson was there like an old friend to meet it, and meet it he most definitely did, I am happy to say."

"I happen to believe that Jerry Talbot was innocent of the crime of which he was accused."

"You are entitled to believe what you choose to believe. *I* happen to believe that Mel would not act without due and just cause. Talbot threatened to kill Denby. Mel told me he was on hand and heard the boy make the threat against that gambler Denby.

"You know Mel Bronson, Jessica, as well as I do. He is not a man given to rash judgments or precipitate behavior. I have done business with Mel for many years. Most recently, he was good enough to take a chattel mortgage on my cattle when I suddenly ran into unexpected financial difficulties. When the bank would not even consider my application for a loan, Mel was there for me. He stepped into the breach and saved me from what could well have become, in a relatively short time, financial ruin."

Jessie wondered what all that had to do with Mel Bronson and his vigilantes conducting a lynching party with Moses Slater as the guest of honor, but she did not say so out loud.

Instead, she said, "When did the—event—take place, Vincent?"

"Two days ago. Moses Slater was in town and, I hear, had been drinking in the Last Chance Saloon. Evelyn said he followed her home and forced himself upon her."

"You were not home at the time?"

"No, I was at business as usual at that time of day. I did not arrive home until after six o'clock—again as usual. I would not be here today were it not for the fact that I fear to leave Evelyn alone. She needs my support at this critical time in her life. I only wish her mother, God rest her soul, were here to help her. A woman's touch is needed at a time like this."

"I'll stop by tomorrow if I may, Vincent," Jessie said. "Please tell Evelyn I was here."

"Promise me you won't upset her. If you do, I shall have to ask you to leave."

"I just want to find out what happened. I'm sure you can understand that, Vincent. I still find it almost impossible to believe that Moses Slater would do what he has been accused of doing."

"I know you and Slater have been good friends over the years," Pruitt said, rising to signal that the discussion was about at an end. "I also know he worked for your father years ago."

"He was always a good employee and a good friend."

"There is something you should bear in mind, Jessica. People change. They do not merely grow older in many cases; they change. Slater changed. But then, thinking back, maybe he was always the randy animal he proved himself to be with my poor Evelyn."

"What do you mean?" Jessica asked, also rising and walking out into the foyer.

"You know that Slater had a romance with a woman some years ago and that he fully intended to marry her. He bought her a very expensive diamond ring, as I recall. He talked to everyone about the end of his affair once it fell apart. Joked about it, in fact. Said he meant to keep the ring forever to remind himself of what he was pleased to call his youthful folly. I wonder now if the woman who jilted him didn't show good sense in doing so. It may well be that she saw his proclivities then and wanted no part of them or him."

Speculation, Jessie thought as Pruitt opened the front door for her. Speculation pure and simple. "Good-bye, Vincent."

The door closed.

"So you think something's rotten in the state of Denmark, do you?" Ki asked that night after dinner as he and Jessie sat in the lamplit great room.

"I'm not sure. It's just that I can't get it through my head that Moses Slater could commit rape. On the other hand, I can think of no real good reason why Evelyn Pruitt would lie about such a thing."

"Nor can I."

"I know. You think I'm being foolish."

"It's never foolish to examine a problem from every possible angle in the search for a solution."

"I wonder what it was he wanted to talk to me about."

"There's no telling at this point."

"You told me he said it was something important."

Ki nodded.

Jessie took a sip from her glass and stared pensively through the window at the darkness outside. After a long moment: "I wonder if you would do something for me."

"Sure, I would. What is it?"

"I'm going into town again tomorrow, as I told you earlier, to try to have a talk with Evelyn Pruitt about what supposedly happened to her."

Ki arched an eyebrow. "What 'supposedly' happened to her?"

"I can't—or maybe I just won't—believe that Moses raped her. But to get back to the favor I have in mind. I'd like you to go and have a talk with Janice Drake. You know Janice rather well, I believe."

"Rather well," Ki admitted.

"How long were you two . . . good friends?"

"Close to a year. The courtship was a hot and heavy one toward the end. I suppose it was too hot and too heavy. It sort of burned itself out. Why do you want me to have a talk with Janice?"

"I don't know really. It's just that I have the fond but rather faint hope that you might be able to discover something about Jerry's and Mel Bronson's relationships with her which might tie in with Jerry's murder."

"That's stretching things pretty far, isn't it, Jessie? I mean the fact that two men are interested in the same woman doesn't mean that one of them would take a notion to get rid—permanently—of his rival. That is what you're thinking might have happened, isn't it?"

Jessie admitted, somewhat ruefully, that it was. "Ugly things have been known to happen when the green-eyed monster, otherwise known as jealousy, rears its ugly head."

Ki finished his drink and put his glass down. "Well, if it will make you happy, I'll go and talk to Janice in the morning."

"And I'll talk to Evelyn Pruitt."

"Maybe one or the other of us will come up with something helpful."

"I'm sincerely hoping so," Jessie said somberly. "I've made a vow to myself that I am going to investigate the killings committed by the Vigilance Committee in the hope of preventing any more from occurring by proving that one— maybe more—of their victims was actually innocent. Tomorrow, with your help, maybe I'll be able to do just that."

After breakfast the next morning, Jessie and Ki rode into town together, separating at the intersection of Main and Pine Streets, as Ki headed for the home of Janice Drake and Jessie went in the opposite direction to pay a return visit to the Pruitt household.

When Ki arrived at the Drake house, he found Janice seated in the porch swing drinking a glass of lemonade. She jumped up when she saw him dismount and tie his horse to a gatepost.

"Hello, there, Ki," she chirped as he came up the walk to the porch. "How are you?"

136

"Fine, Janice. Yourself?"

"Feeling fit as a fiddle. Come and sit down. No, not there. Here. On the swing." Janice sat down and patted the empty space beside her on the swing. When Ki had seated himself next to her, she asked, "It's as hot as a furnace, isn't it? Would you like a glass of lemonade?"

"I'll have a sip of yours, if you don't mind."

"Help yourself," a smiling Janice said, proffering her half-filled glass.

Ki put his hand around hers that was holding the glass, raised the glass to his lips, his eyes on Janice's, and drank.

"That's good," he commented, releasing his hold on her hand.

"It's not too sweet?"

"It's just right."

"To what do I owe the unexpected pleasure of your company?"

"I'd been thinking about you and thought I'd stop by and say howdy," Ki answered, telling almost the whole truth. "I hope you're glad I did."

"You know I'm always glad to see you, Ki. I'm so pleased we can still be friends even if we're not—well, what we once were to each other."

"So am I. I hear you have no shortage of gentlemen callers there days. Mel Bronson and Jerry Talbot—the late Jerry Talbot, I should say—to name but two."

"Wasn't that terrible, what happened to poor dear Jerry?"

"It most certainly was. I imagine you were devastated when you heard the news."

"Well, of course I was. Anyone would be, wouldn't they? I mean, Jerry and I were—more than friends, you know."

"It must have been particularly difficult for you knowing that one of your other admirers had a hand in Jerry's death."

Janice hung her head, her blond sausage curls shadowing her face. "Life is a funny thing, isn't it?" she murmured. "To think that Mel should be one of the men who shot Jerry

137

down. Mel felt terrible about what happened too."

"How do you know?"

"He told me. He said he had always thought Jerry Talbot was as law-abiding as the day was long. He never thought Jerry had it in him to kill another man like he did that gambler Denby."

"Jerry told Jessie and me before the vigilantes gunned him down that he didn't kill Denby."

"Did he? Well, I'm not surprised really."

"You're not?"

"Why, no. After all, he wouldn't be liable to just stand up and declare for all and sundry to hear that he was guilty as charged, now would he?"

"Are you still seeing Mel Bronson?"

Janice raised her head and gave Ki a shy smile. She nodded.

He matched her smile, his a sly one. "Are you sure his intentions are honorable?"

Janice blushed prettily. "What an awful thing to say! Shame on you. Of course his intentions are honorable. Mel's a fine upstanding gentleman."

"I could use another sip of your lemonade, if you don't mind."

As Janice gave it to Ki, she said, "Sometimes the terrible things that happen to a person in life turn out in the end to be blessings in disguise."

Ki watched Janice expectantly, waiting for her to go on.

"I mean, when Jerry and Mel were both coming to call on me, I was in a dither, I confess to you. I sometimes didn't know which way to turn or what to do. It's a terrible thing, I told Mel one time, to be in love with two men at the same time."

"You told Bronson you loved him and Jerry?"

"Yes. Equally was the way I put it, as I recall. I loved them both equally, I told Mel, and I simply could not make up my mind between them. Mel kept urging me to choose, but I swear to you, Ki, I simply couldn't, though I tried most valiantly to do so. At times, he became quite cross with me as a result."

138

"Because you wouldn't come down on his side, you mean."

"Yes, that's it exactly." Janice giggled. "I'll tell you a secret. I used to have a terrible time of it keeping those two apart. It got to the point that when Jerry was with me I was on pins and needles for fear that Mel would arrive on the scene. And then, when Mel and I were alone together, I was on the same pins and needles and sick with worry that Jerry would put in an unexpected appearance. That kind of thing can wear a girl down to a nub in less time than it takes to tell about it, Ki, I do declare."

"I'm sure you're right. I take it neither man had any love for the other."

"To put it mildly. They were like two dogs made mad, each of them, by the simple sight of the other. They were always on the verge of going for each other's throats."

"It was that bad, huh?"

"Well, I am exaggerating a teeny-weeny little bit. I mean, they never actually had words and they never did come to blows over me, but if the three of us ever turned out to be in the same place at the same time, as happened more than once—well, the air quickly became so cold you could have chipped it with a knife as if it were a block of ice. There was most certainly no love lost between the two of them, Mel and Jerry."

Ki now thought he understood what Janice had meant about earlier when she referred to "blessings in disguise." "I suppose things have gotten a bit easier for you since Jerry's untimely demise. In terms of the love rivalry, I mean."

Janice looked away. She bit her lower lip for a moment and then said, with her voice trembling, "I know you must think I'm awful for saying—for even daring to think— such a thing." Defiantly: "But it's true, so why shouldn't I say it?"

"No reason in the world, I reckon."

"When I heard that Jerry was dead, I was crushed. At first. But then, as the days passed and Mel continued courting me, I came to realize how my life had suddenly become so much simpler. So much less vexing. I no longer was torn to pieces

139

by my love for the two of them. I was almost content, you might say. Oh, that sounds simply awful. I can't seem to find the right words to say precisely what I mean."

"I think I understand what you're saying."

"It was as if a great burden had suddenly been lifted from these all-too-frail shoulders of mine. As if the choice had been made for me. Taken right out of my hands. Oh, I still miss Jerry. He was such a wonderful person and such a sweet-talking man." Janice blushed. "He had a boyish way about him and he was a man who could charm bees out of their hive and almost any woman in the world into his arms. I shall miss him, I suppose, for the remaining days of my life."

"But you still have Mel Bronson, which surely must be some consolation."

"Oh, he has been a comfort to me in my time of travail, Ki. He most certainly has been. At first—I hope you won't think I am being prideful when I say this. At first, Mel was just not himself. He felt terrible about Jerry's death. I told him that he had done what had to be done. After all, Jerry Talbot had gone bad. Become a killer. He'd had to be stopped before he killed again. I tried my best to console Mel, and I finally succeeded. He listened to my advice, and has now managed to put the whole unsightly business behind him. We go on now, the two of us, almost as if nothing had happened. Mel says if it hadn't been for me and my help he doesn't know what he would have done, he was so heartsore over having to shoot Jerry."

"He and his vigilantes have been busy of late, there's no getting around that fact. We've had a whole bunch of hangings, thanks to them."

"I know. But the world—our town—is a safer place to live in as a result. There aren't men like that awful Moses Slater on the loose now. Or if there are, they have had fair warning not to indulge their evil instincts.

"Of course, Mel is about worn out between the demands of his private life and those arising from what he sees as his public duty as head of the Vigilance Committee. Some evenings when he comes to call he is plumb tuckered. It tears at my heart to see him so, but when I chide him and tell him he must slow down, he chucks me under the chin and smiles that come-hither smile of his and tells me he has obligations that cannot be denied. Did I tell you that he has asked me to marry him?"

Ki shook his head.

"Yes, he has. Of course, that is not the first time he has popped the question, as people say." Janice tossed her curls and continued. "He has asked me, oh, I don't know how many times to be his blushing bride. I could never bring myself to say yes before."

"Why was that?"

"I thought I had explained all that. It was because of Jerry. When I was also seeing Jerry—I couldn't make up my mind between the two of them. I was torn between Jerry and Mel and it was, as I've said, a most distressing situation. But now—"

"Now the coast is clear for Mel with Jerry permanently out of the running."

Janice gave Ki a speculative look, her brow furrowing. "You put things rather crudely, I must say."

"But truthfully, I think."

"You don't sound one bit happy for me and my newfound good fortune."

"You're talking about your planned marriage to Mel Bronson." When Janice, on the verge of pouting, nodded, Ki added, "I congratulate you both. I hope you'll be very happy together."

"That's much better!" Janice cried as she put down her glass and girlishly clapped her hands in delight. "Now you sound like the old Ki, the one I knew ages ago. Have you found anyone you liked better than me since then?"

"I've been out with one or two nice ladies." Ki rose. "It's been good talking to you again, Janice."

"Don't be such a stranger!" she called after him as he made his way to his horse, stepped into the saddle, and rode down the street.

Rivalry.

141

The word hummed in Ki's mind. There most certainly had been a distinct and on-going rivalry between Mel Bronson and Jerry Talbot for the affections of Janice Drake. But was it a sufficient motive for foul play on the part of one romantic rival against the other, to give the survivor a clear field? Ki didn't think so, and intended to tell Jessie so when they next met. And yet . . .

His speculations were sidetracked when he caught sight of a familiar face at the stage station on the west side of town. He rode up to Dolores Warner and gave her a warm smile and greeting.

"Oh, it's you, Ki. Hello. How are you?"

"Fine, Mrs. Warner. Taking a trip, are you, or are you meeting someone on the incoming stage?"

"I'm not meeting anyone. I'm taking the stage to San Antonio."

"I hope you will have a pleasant visit. San Antonio is a bustling—some say a brawling—town. Full of excitement."

"I'm not visiting there. I plan to stay there for a spell with my sister and her husband, that's true, but then I'll be moving on. I'm really not sure where to at this time."

"You're pulling up stakes here?"

"Yes. I could no longer hold on to the homeplace. Perhaps you didn't know—Bob and I tried to keep our personal business private as much as possible—but we had been having financial difficulties for some time before the vigilantes hanged him. With him gone, there was no way I could hold on to the place.

"Bob went to the bank but Mr. Traynor there, he wouldn't lend us another dime to help us keep our heads above water. In fact, he said he'd been carrying us for far too long as it was and that wasn't good business for the bank. He told us he was going to have to foreclose if we couldn't come up with the money we owed him and his bank.

"Well, we couldn't. Then Bob—died. The bank has foreclosed as Mr. Traynor said they would, and I have to leave and start a new life somewheres else, though how in the world is a sixty-year-old woman like me going to do a thing like that at my stage in life, for pity's sake? Neither Mr. Traynor nor anybody else, I reckon, can answer me that."

Ki stared at the woman who stood there looking up at him, clearly bewildered. His heart went out to her.

"I have to ask you to forgive me, you and Jessie," Dolores Warner went on, "for not coming by to tell you I was leaving. But it seemed to me—it just seemed so hard a thing to do I couldn't break myself to the bit and go on and do it. It's not easy bidding good-bye to friends you've known for so many years, good strong friends like you and Jessie. Like I said, I just couldn't make myself do it. I suppose I thought deep down in my heart of hearts if I didn't actually say it—good-bye, I mean—it would be almost like not really losing the friendships that were so precious to me."

"I'm sorry, Mrs. Warner, about all that has happened."

"Oh, I don't want pity. Maybe after all it's time for me to be moving on." She tried a smile that didn't work. "Maybe I'll get lucky and meet some well-heeled gentleman up in San Antonio and he'll take a shine to me. Well, it's possible, isn't it? There's never a goose so gray, they say, who can't find herself a gander."

Ki couldn't help admiring the bravado Dolores Warner was so gamely displaying while the tears were simultaneously welling up in her eyes and about to undo her. To spare her that humiliation, he asked, "Who was it bought your property?"

"I don't rightly know."

"You don't know?"

"Mr. Traynor at the bank, he said it was bought by some business interests, but he didn't give me a name. Not that it matters. It's good land. It's got good water. If we had a little more time we might have made it, Bob and me. Well, the Lord is still my shepherd, though he does work sometimes in mysterious and, I can testify, truly trying ways.

"Oh, here it comes, the stage." Dolores Warner bent down and picked up the small cloth satchel that sat at her feet as the stage rumbled down the street toward her and Ki.

"I'd best get out of the way," Ki said, "if I don't want to get run down. I'll say good-bye to you now, Mrs. Warner, and wish you the very best of luck in the future."

She took the hand he offered her and gently shook it. "You be sure to tell Jessie you saw me, won't you, Ki? You'll be sure to tell her why I didn't come by to bid her farewell?"

"I will."

"Good-bye then."

Ki walked his horse from out in front of the stage station as the stage pulled up in a cloud of thick dust, which caused the horses pulling the stage to snort and slobber.

He glanced back over his shoulder as he continued riding down the street, and saw Dolores Warner climb into the coach and disappear from sight.

Moments later, after the driver had climbed back aboard the coach, it moved out, harness jingling merrily, horses straining at their traces. As the coach passed Ki, he waved, although he could not actually see Mrs. Warner inside the vehicle. The coach rounded the corner up ahead of him, nearly turning over as it did so because of the intense speed at which it was traveling.

"Yoo-hoo! Ki, up here, honey!"

The lilting feminine voice sent a thrill through Ki as he recognized it. He looked up and saw the melon-breasted Dixie Sinclair leaning at a precarious angle out of the window of Mrs. Palmer's parlor house and waving to him with both beringed hands.

He touched the brim of his hat to her and gave her a grin.

A smile blazed on Dixie's somewhat broad but nevertheless pretty face. She was a petite woman who barely filled the window through which she was so eagerly leaning. Her hair was a bright blond, corn silk in the sun. Her eyes were blue, bits of sky in white seas. They sparkled now, and her full lips, parted and glistening, were altogether alluring. As was the compact lushness of all the rest of her.

"You're not going to just ride on by without stopping to say howdy, are you now?"

Dixie's words had been, it seemed to Ki, both a subtle invitation and a not-so-subtle challenge. He made up his mind on the spot to promptly accept both the invitation and the challenge.

"I'm on my way," he called back with a wave, "with my hat thrown back and my spurs a-jingling."

Dixie gave a delighted giggle and vanished from the window. She opened the door of the parlor house a moment before Ki, who had left his horse at the hitch rail out front, could knock upon it. She seized him by the arm and pulled him inside as if fearful that, if she didn't, he might change his mind—or escape from her.

She threw her arms around him and kissed him squarely on his mouth, her tongue breaching the twin barriers of his lips and teeth. Then she held him out in front of her at arm's length and remarked, "How're they hanging, honey?"

Ki was not at all taken aback by Dixie's bawdiness. It was, he thought, refreshing. Where other people tiptoed tentatively around the subject of sex, Dixie leaped into it with both feet and not a moment's hesitation or false modesty.

"Don't bother to answer," she said. "I intend to find out the answer for my own self. Come on upstairs and you and me'll set about making the two-backed beast. Unless, that is, you have something else in mind."

The Pruitt house was quiet when Jessie knocked on its front door. A lace curtain drifted on the breeze in an open window. The fence gate swung in the same breeze, creaking its need for oil.

The door opened and Evelyn Pruitt, looking drawn and pale, smiled weakly and said, "Daddy told me you were here yesterday, Jessie. I'm sorry I couldn't see you then, but I was a bit under the weather. I still am, to tell you the truth."

"I hope you don't mind my stopping by like this."

Evelyn pressed her lips together and her eyes wavered, unable or unwilling to meet Jessie's own.

Fearful that Evelyn's hesitation and shifting gaze signaled her intent to send her away with her questions unasked, Jessie stepped boldly forward.

145

"Shall we go inside? It's hot out here."

"Oh, yes. Of course. Do come in."

Jessie went through the foyer and into the parlor, where she sat down in the same chair she had sat in the day before when she talked to Evelyn's father, Vincent. He was now nowhere in sight.

"Daddy went to his office," Evelyn volunteered as she also sat down. "He wanted to remain at home here with me, but I insisted he go to work. I can't be a burden to him forever, can I?"

"He's been very concerned about your well-being. He told me so, although he didn't have to. I know your father idolizes you and worries about you. It must have been almost as much of a shock to him, what happened, as it was to you."

Evelyn looked about the room as if searching for something, Jessie thought. Or perhaps she was making sure that no rapist was lurking in any of the room's shadowy corners.

When she spoke again, her voice was distinct but faint. "Sometimes I think I dreamed it all. Sometimes I think I will wake up at any moment and it will all be over. Just a foolish dream, a dark night's fancy. But I know in my heart of hearts that that will never happen. In my heart of hearts I know I was attacked and unspeakable things were done to me by that . . . that . . ."

When Evelyn's words trailed away into a stark silence, Jessie said,. "I was shocked when I heard what had happened. Shocked in part, I confess, because Moses Slater was an old and dear friend of mine."

Evelyn's head swung around. She stared at Jessie her eyes vague, almost empty.

"I'd known Moses since I was a child," Jessie continued. "I'd never known him, in all that time, to do anything the least bit lawless. Why, he would never even cheat at cards. I remember how the other men in the bunkhouse would tease him about that. They would ask him how he expected to get by in a dog-eat-dog world unless he learned to play with a deck containing five aces. Moses would just smile and say he was sure he'd get along well enough walking the straight and narrow. The day he had to take up cheating to win, he'd say, would be the day he'd rather stop playing cards. So you see how hard it was for me to accept what had happened."

Evelyn's eyes narrowed. "What you really mean is that you found it hard to believe that what happened did indeed happen."

"In a sense, yes."

"It *did* happen. I didn't imagine it."

"Evelyn, I'd like to ask you something. It might upset you so I'm warning you of that possibility in advance. If you would rather I didn't ask you, I'll not."

Evelyn's body seemed to stiffen. "I don't believe I could be more upset than I already am."

"Did you do anything—anything at all—that might have caused Moses Slater to believe that you sought his attentions?"

Evelyn's eyes widened in surprise. "Of course I didn't. What kind of a woman do you think I am? I'm not one of those soiled doves who work in Mrs. Palmer's parlor house. I did nothing to encourage him to attend to me in any way whatsoever. I merely met him in town and when he greeted me, I responded. We exchanged 'good days,' that is all."

"And then he followed you home."

"He must have. Although I didn't notice him do so."

"When you arrived home—"

"I put my packages away and then went out to the barn to see how my mare, Bess, was doing. She'd had colic of late and we had to have Doctor Ives come and take a look at her. I was standing just outside Bess's stall when I saw a shadow fall on the floor. I thought at first that Daddy had come home early. I turned—but it was him!"

"Moses Slater."

"Yessss!" Evelyn hissed.

"Then what happened?"

"Must I answer these questions? I'd really rather not, you know."

"Did he attack you then?"

Again, a sibilant *"Yessss!"*

"Did he say anything before he did so?"

"Something about me being a—a pretty package. Those were his words. 'Pretty package.' He leered at me."

"And it was then that he attacked you."

Evelyn nodded and lowered her head. Her fingers danced nervously in her lap.

"When it was over—what happened then?"

"What do you mean what happened then?" a tense Evelyn asked, looking up again at Jessie. "He buttoned his trousers and left."

"Leaving you—where?"

"Where? On the floor. In the dirt and straw, that's where. What is this, Jessie? A new form of the Inquisition you're conducting? Does all this titillate you? Is that it? Or are you trying to prove that I am making the story up so that your precious friend—that *monster* Moses Slater—can be rehabilitated, at least in your memory?"

"I'm truly sorry if I've upset you, Evelyn, I guess it's partly true that I was hoping against hope that nothing had really happened. That—"

"It *did* happen!"

"I was hoping that—well, never mind. I was told you went to Mel Bronson to report the outrage committed against you."

"I did. I was almost distraught. I *was* distraught. But—but, yes, I went to Mr. Bronson."

"Why?"

"Why? Because he and the other members of the Vigilance Committee have been cleaning up the town and surrounding countryside. I wanted them to punish Moses Slater for what he had done to me. I wanted vengeance!"

And you got it, Jessie thought. In spades, you got it.

"Why didn't you report the incident to Marshal Collins instead?"

Evelyn huffed disdainfully. "Marshal Collins is the poorest excuse for a lawman I've ever seen in all my born days. That's why."

"I see."

"Do you? Good. Then you'll be on your way, I presume." Evelyn rose. "I'll show you to the door."

148

★

Chapter 9

Dixie pulled down the shades in her bedroom and then wrapped her arms around Ki and kissed him hard.

He returned her kiss, feeling himself stiffen rapidly as he did so. They stood there, for a long moment locked in their embrace, the heat of their joined bodies gradually increasing. Then Dixie drew away from him, breathing deeply to catch her breath.

"You haven't changed a bit," she whispered, placing the tip of a playful index finger on the end of his nose. "You're always hot to trot."

"You're not?"

"I'm paid to be."

"I'm disappointed," Ki said, taking her finger and nibbling it with his teeth. "I thought you were all warmed up because of your unbridled lust for me."

"That's a big part of it. Does that make you feel better?"

He nipped her finger and she let out a howl of mock outrage. Then moving into the circle of his arms again, she slid the fingers of one hand beneath his shirt and began to explore his chest.

He sighed under her delicate ministrations. Her hand was warm and her fingernails cool. They tickled. They also tweaked his nipples. Dixie's other hand slid down along his body and came to rest between his legs, where it cozily cupped his genitals. She squeezed them lightly, and then softly caressed them through the cloth of his trousers. He responded in kind, first fondling her breasts and then her hot mound, which she thrust at him with a provocative twitch of her agile pelvis.

"You're hard as a rock," she whispered. "Just the way I like my men. I don't mean just your you-know-what. I mean your whole body. It's all muscle."

Dixie moved away from him. She pulled her dress over her head with a soft swishing sound. Underneath it she was naked. When she approached him again, his hands eagerly explored the seductive landscape of her young body. He estimated Dixie's age at no more than eighteen. She had soft breasts, rounded hips, and firm thighs and calves.

He began to undress, fumbling with the buttons on his shirt and jeans, his breath beginning to come in excited gusts. Dixie helped him by pulling off his boots and tossing his hat onto a nearby chair. When he was as naked as she was, she lay down on the bed and drew him down upon her.

She spread her legs and adjusted her pelvis as Ki, one hand gripping his jutting erection, guided it into her warmth and wetness. When he was all the way within her, he lay motionless on her for a brief moment, kissing her cheeks and nuzzling her neck. He let himself experience the arousing sensation of her lush breasts pressing against his chest, let himself feel imprisoned by her as she wrapped her legs around his thighs, exulted in the heat of the fire she had kindled within him. As that fire burned brighter and hotter, he raised his hips slightly, lowered them, and groaned with pleasure as her nimble fingers ran up and down his spine to send shivers coursing through him.

He began slowly, maintaining an easy but steady rhythm, until she began to respond and move eagerly beneath him. Then he increased the speed of his steady thrusting, plunging deep within her and delighting in the way her hips lunged upward to meet his, fell away, lunged again.

As Dixie's body melded with his own in an ecstatic union that brought him an increasing sense of exhilaration, his arms went under and around her as if to draw her even closer to him, although he knew he could not possibly do so.

Their lips met. Their tongues explored.

Dixie pulled away, throwing her head back and arching her neck. With her legs still clinging tightly to him, she began to emit a series of grunts, which were quickly followed by a long drawn-out sigh as she climaxed and her moist breath warmed his neck.

He felt the world begin to shrink around him, and when it became centered in his loins, his bucking and rearing reached a crescendo as he felt himself explode and heard Dixie cry out wordlessly, her fingernails clawing his bare back as her cry faded away and she lay passively beneath him.

When his body finally quieted and was once more under control, he pulled his arms out from under her. Using his hands to frame her face, he called her sweet names and paid her breathless compliments.

Her legs withdrew from his and she brought them together under his, her hands sliding down his sweaty spine to come to rest upon his buttocks. She held him pressed tightly against her. Ki neither knew nor cared how much time had passed before Dixie stirred and then rolled her hips in a tantalizing way that immediately roused him into instant action once again.

When at last it ended for them and he had withdrawn from her, he flopped down beside her, his right hand holding her left hand. For a time, there was only the sound of their heavy breathing in the room as Ki, more than merely satisfied, let himself drift and dream of the sense-shattering pleasure that had just been his.

"You deserve a prize," Dixie remarked languidly as she lay next to him. "A medal maybe."

"I do? For what?"

"They give them, don't they, to top-notch stallions? At county fairs and such? You could enter one of those contests at the Harvest Home Festival this fall. I know you'd win, hands down."

Ki rode whistling out of town some time later, visions of a particular sugarplum—Dixie—dancing in his head and still stirring lust in his groin, though he was both spent and satisfied after his recent encounter with her at Mrs. Palmer's parlor house.

He thought of how she had said she felt guilty charging him two dollars for what they had done.

"I almost feel like I should be paying *you*," she had sheepishly said.

But he'd insisted on paying, saying, "A working girl deserves to be remunerated for services rendered. Especially when those services were rendered so skillfully."

Dixie, obviously delighted by his remark, gave one of her characteristic little yelps and flew at him. As her feet left the floor, he managed to catch her—just barely. She threw her arms around his neck and smothered him with kisses until he finally put her down and left.

His whistling stopped as he let out an involuntary guffaw at the memory. Then he resumed his whistling and rode on, traveling north on the stage road. He had gone less than a mile through brush country when he spotted Jessie riding up ahead of him.

I'm one lucky man, he told himself, spurring his horse in order to catch up with her. I encounter two beautiful women in the space of one hour. I'm twice blessed.

"Jessie!" he called out as he neared her. When she turned and saw him, she waved and he returned her wave.

"I thought you'd probably be home by now," he said when he reached her. "I'm afraid I dawdled awhile in town." Was that what he had done with Dixie? Dawdled? He almost laughed out loud.

"I stopped at Mrs. Clancy's," Jessie said as they rode on together. "But first I went to the dry goods store and they had the most magnificent material that had just come in from New York City. I couldn't resist it. It was green satin. It matched the color of my eyes perfectly. So I bought yards and yards of it and took it to Mrs. Clancy to make me a party gown out of it. I intend to be the smartest-looking woman at the next party I go to thanks to that lovely green satin. Mrs. Clancy is going to put frills on the hems and bodice and she says this gown will be her pièce de résistance."

"I didn't know you were planning on going to a party."

"I wasn't. I mean, none is being held that I know of or was invited to. But I'll tell you this. If I don't get invited to somebody's party when Mrs. Clancy finishes making my dress, *I'll* have a party just to show off my gown."

Ki smiled. "Did you get to talk to Evelyn Pruitt?"

"Yes, I did. How about you? Did you see Janice Drake?"

"I saw her."

"Did you learn anything significant?"

"Not really, no. She did freely admit to having been romantically involved with both Mel Bronson and Jerry Talbot. But we knew that. She said she was shocked at the news—and manner—of Talbot's death. She also said that apparently Bronson was too. She said he felt guilty about what had happened."

"I find that difficult to believe."

Ki shrugged. "I'm only telling you what she said during our conversation."

"What else did she have to say?"

"She seemed convinced that Talbot was guilty as charged. It may well be that Bronson has convinced her of that fact in much the same way he convinced himself and the men riding with him of Talbot's guilt. She mentioned that Talbot's death had turned out to be, for her, a blessing in disguise."

Jessie turned her head and stared at Ki in shocked surprise.

"With Talbot dead, she felt her problem—the love rivalry she found herself tangled up in—had ended."

"Giving Mel Bronson a clear field with her."

"Yes."

"Did she, by any chance, report bad blood between her two suitors?"

153

"I don't know if it was bad blood she talked about. That may well be too strong a term to describe the feelings that existed between Talbot and Bronson. But I gathered that they didn't get along all that well when they ran into each other."

"Did they ever come to blows over Janice, did she say?"

"Not according to Janice, they didn't. Jessie, I have to tell you that I don't think there's much of a basis to believe that Bronson set Talbot up for a charge of murder. Nothing Janice told me made me think he would do a thing like that. So he had a rival for the love of his life's affection. It doesn't, in my opinion, follow that he would have made the charge against Talbot just to get him out of the way so he could move in on Janice without interference."

Ki noticed the look of disappointment that clouded Jessie's face. "By the way, Bronson has asked Janice to marry him and she's said yes to his proposal, which, I gather, was not unexpected."

"There it is," Jessie said. "Bronson wins the fair lady by eliminating his rival for her hand."

Ki hesitated a moment before saying, "I think you're jumping to an unwarranted conclusion, Jessie. You're losing sight of the fact that Talbot did say in my presence that he intended to kill that gambler Denby. Bronson was there. He heard him. So when Denby winds up shot to death—well, who would you choose as the most likely suspect in the killing given the circumstances—the threat Talbot openly made against Denby in the presence of witnesses, myself and Mel Bronson among them?"

Jessie remained silent, the look of disappointment back on her face.

Ki went on. "I know you and Talbot and his brother, Bud, were good friends since you were children together. Maybe you're letting that fact and the emotion that goes with it cloud your judgment in this matter, Jessie."

"Maybe," she grudgingly admitted after a moment, but said no more as they rode on.

"In any event," Ki continued, "you're not going to be able to prove that Bronson set Talbot up by anything Janice Drake has said or is likely to say in the future. Even if she found out that Bronson did indeed manage to get rid of his rival in their affair of the heart, she isn't likely to say so in light of the fact that she's going to marry the man—"

"Look!"

Ki looked to the north, the direction in which Jessie had pointed, and saw a stagecoach careening toward them. The driver was lashing his horses as he bent forward in the driver's seat, and the man riding shotgun beside him fired his rifle over the top of the coach at the three pursuing men.

"Highway robbers," Jessie said. "Let's put a stop to them!"

Without waiting for a response from Ki, she raked her horse's flanks with her spurs and went galloping toward the stage, drawing the gun she was wearing strapped around her waist as she did so.

Ki went after her, riding hard.

Rifle shots continued to sound, as did rounds fired by the three men chasing the stage. Jessie pointed to her left and Ki, understanding her meaning, rode that way as she angled off to the right. Both of them left the stage road clear behind them as they circled around, intending to come in on the flanks of the would-be robbers.

The stage rocked from side to side as it hit bumps in the rutted road. A woman passenger leaned out one of its open windows and proceeded to be sick. A short man wearing a derby hat was visible in another window as he held onto his hat and his eyes widened in fright. The man's eyes widened even more as two of the stage's pursuers pulled up on either side of the vehicle and fired the sixguns in their hands.

The woman who had been leaning out the window jerked her head back inside. Above her, the man riding shotgun threw up his hands as he was hit and fell to the ground with his weapon.

The stage rattled on, its driver's face white with fear.

A shot sounded and the driver stood up, swayed for a moment, and then toppled to the ground. He was dragged by the reins in his hands for a short distance before the reins ripped free as the stage sped on, the team pulling it galloping unchecked now at breakneck speed.

Jessie wheeled her horse and made a beeline for the stage. She squeezed off a shot, which nicked one of the highwaymen in the shoulder, causing him to curse and return her fire.

His shot whined past Jessie's left ear, almost singeing her hair as it did so. She fired another round at her assailant, but this time she missed.

The man who had been riding on the other side of the stage circled around behind it to see what had happened to his opposite number.

"She shot me!" his companion yelled at the top of his voice, and pointed at Jessie.

The man who had joined him fired at her. His shot grazed her horse's neck, causing it to scream and its gait to falter. Jessie grabbed a fistful of the animal's mane to help her stay in the saddle as she tightened her grip on the reins and her mount fought the bit, its head tossing wildly as blood oozed from its wounded neck.

She managed to turn the animal—just in time. A volley of shots, fired at her by all three highwaymen, missed because they had been sent burning through the air toward the spot where she had been a moment before.

She caught a glimpse of Ki on the far side of the coach, which was continuing to roar along the road, completely out of control. As she rode behind a pile of broken boulders littering the side of the road, she saw Ki turn his horse and begin to ride parallel to the stage. The passengers had begun to shout for help and, in the case of the woman, to scream. As she brought her horse to a skidding halt, she saw Ki stand up in his stirrups, leap into the air, and land on the back of one of the pair of horses leading the team.

Jessie lost sight of him when gunfire from the three highwaymen forced her out of the saddle and down to the ground, where she took cover behind one of the boulders. With her back pressed up against it, she thumbed cartridges out of her belt loops and loaded the empty chambers of her gun's cylinder. Then turning around again, she was startled to see three other riders heading in her direction. They were too far away for her to recognize them at first, but then, as they came closer, she saw with an odd mixture of relief and apprehension that the riders were Mel Bronson, Jim Bob Simpson, and Charles Proctor.

Vigilantes!

Ki struggled to stay where he was, on the back of the horse that was one half of the two-horse team leading the other two members of the team as they all galloped wildly on their way to no known destination.

The task was an exceedingly difficult one, given the bouncing of the horse's body, which sent bone-shaking tremors through Ki's body, and also given the fact that the horse's hide was sweat-soaked and thus slippery. He gripped it tightly with his knees and seized some of its mane with his left hand. With his right hand, he made a grab for the slack reins that were dropping low—almost to the horse's hocks.

Out of reach. He swore and bent to the right, using the sweaty slipperiness of the horse's hide to his advantage as he reached down and tried again to retrieve the reins.

No good. They remained out of reach. He knew he was in danger of slipping too far to the right—and then on down to the ground between the two lead horses to be crushed to death by them and those behind them.

He tried again to reach the reins, his left foot hooked in the traces to try to keep himself from falling from his precarious perch. He stretched his arm down as far as it would go—and still farther. The reins remained out of reach. He finally gave up on his attempt to retrieve the reins, and pulled himself up until he was once again in a sitting position. He was only vaguely aware of the female screams coming from inside the coach behind him and the garbled cries and shouts of the male passengers. He was not at all aware of the landscape flashing past him—trees, mesas, and vast stretches of grassland.

There was only one thing he could think of to do that might, just might, help him achieve his goal of halting the runaway horses. Without hesitation, he did it. Bracing both feet in the traces to steady himself as best he could under the dangerous circumstances, he rose, his buttocks leaving the horse's back. At the same time, he raised his free right hand, which he had formed into a fist. Leaning forward, he brought it slamming down on the head of the horse he was straddling, striking the animal a savage blow right between the eyes.

The horse ran on without missing a step.

Ki hit it again, and then again, with a hammering series of blows. They slowed but did not stop the animal. When he changed his tactics slightly and struck the horse, first in one eye and then in the other, he achieved his desperate goal.

The horse halted. Or tried to. But the other horse directly behind it collided with it, pushing it forward. The horse in the lead shook its head and dug in its forefeet. It screamed in pain. Its companion was forcibly slowed by its refusal to move any more than it was forced to.

Ki reached out and seized the bit of the horse on his right. He jerked it hard. Once. Twice. Blood began to mix with the saliva dribbling from the horse's mouth as the iron bit broke the skin of its lips.

Ki held onto the bit, twisting it back and forth to cause the horse more pain.

His efforts finally met with the success he had been struggling to attain. Now both lead horses refused to budge. Thus, the two behind them had no recourse but to stop.

The woman in the coach stopped screaming as it rocked to an abrupt halt.

"We've stopped!" a man shouted. "Thank God, we've finally stopped!"

Ki slid down from the back of the horse he had been riding and walked around to the door of the coach, which he opened.

"You folks had better step down in case those critters pulling this thing decided to take off at a run again."

The passengers—a woman and three men—scrambled out of the coach. They all began talking at once as they thanked Ki for what the close-to-hysterical woman called their "deliverance."

He hardly heard her—or any of the men either. His eyes were on the standoff taking place in the distance.

The would-be stagecoach robbers were hunkered down in some thick brush and behind a deadfall. Flashes of gunfire were coming from several other locations. He couldn't see Jessie, and this fact bothered him. Was she one of the people firing at the highwaymen? If so, who were the others?

"Any of you fellows got a gun?" he asked, his eyes still focused on the gunfight and not on the stage passengers.

"Why, yes," one of the men answered hesitantly, "I have a Smith and Wesson .44. But you're not planning to step into the middle of that fracas taking place back there, are you, sir?"

"Give it to me."

"Give it—"

"Your .44," Ki snapped, holding out his hand. "Give it to me."

The man he had spoken to reached under his frock coat and removed his revolver from the shoulder holster he was wearing. He handed it to Ki, who took it and ran for his horse, which was grazing about halfway between the halted stage and the gun battle raging a few hundred yards beyond.

Jessie saw Ki coming and the sight of him made her heart leap, not only because he would soon be with her, but also because he had survived his dangerous attempt to halt the runaway stage. She couldn't resist standing up, although not altogether straight, and waving to him when she saw him heading away from her and realized he had not seen her.

She immediately dropped down again behind the boulder that was affording her cover when he saw her and swerved, galloping now toward her. In what seemed like no time at all, he was drawing rein only a few feet away from her and springing from the saddle to crouch at her side.

"Where did you get that gun?" she asked him.

"From one of the stage passengers. What exactly is going on here?"

159

"The highway men—they're over there." Jessie pointed to the brush and the rotting deadfall not far from it. "Over there—" she pointed again "—there are three vigilantes. Bronson, Simpson, and Charles Proctor."

"They must have been trailing the robbers," Ki speculated. "Or else it was just good luck they came upon them before they could accomplish what they'd set out to do, namely rob the stage."

"I'm not so sure their presence here means good luck for the robbers."

Ki gave Jessie a sidelong glance, and then squeezed off a shot that hit the deadfall and sent wood chips flying up into the air. He ducked down low as his fire was promptly returned.

"Bronson and the others," Jessie said, "if they and we win this gunfight—they'll hang those three men. I'll bet my bottom dollar on it."

"I think that's a safe bet," Ki said grimly as he fired a second shot.

"Look," Jessie said. "The vigilantes are going to rush the robbers' position."

Ki looked and saw that Jessie was right. The three vigilantes had begun to move forward, dashing from tree to boulder to brush as they went. The highwaymen turned defensive fire on the three men moving up on them, leaving Jessie and Ki out of danger for the moment.

"This is our chance," Jessie said. "We can circle around behind those three robbers and get the drop on them. You want to give it a try?"

"I'm game."

"There's something else I intend to do and I could use your help."

"Something else?"

Jessie told her friend what she had in mind, causing him to grin and nod his eager assent to her plan.

"You take the left," Jessie said, "and I'll go to the right. We'll go on foot. We'll make harder-to-hit targets that way. You ready?"

"As I'll ever be."

"Then let's go!"

They went.

As the gun battle between the vigilantes and the highway-men raged, Jessie and Ki circled the position of the latter group and then, after meeting again some two hundred yards beyond the brush and deadfall that were serving the outlaws as a makeshift breastwork, they moved together in silent accord across the rocky ground as they made their silent, stealthy way toward the robbers, their guns drawn and their breaths held.

They were almost within range of the three badmen when Bronson and his two companions suddenly rushed them, their sixguns blazing. The vigilantes overran the robbers' position, and as Jessie and Ki raced up to the six men, they found themselves too late to help in the capture, which, they saw at once, was an already accomplished fact.

Two of the robbers were standing with their hands in the air. The third lay on the ground, blood leaking from a bullet wound in his left cheek and from the exit wound the bullet had left on the man's right temple.

Charles Proctor, also bleeding from a wound in his right thigh, limped forward and, using his good left leg, kicked the man on the ground, rolling him over. He turned to his two companions and, grinning, said, "This one's dead."

"What are you two doing here?" Jim Bob Simpson asked in a tone that suggested he considered Jessie and Ki to be intruders on vigilante territory.

"We might ask you the same thing," Jessie retorted.

"We got a tip," Bronson interjected, locking eyes with her, "that the stage was due to be robbed. We hid out and sure enough, the tip proved to be true. We trailed these three outlaws and, well, you saw the rest, I reckon."

"We were on our way home when we saw them try to rob the stage," Jessie volunteered.

She watched as Proctor disarmed the two highwaymen and tossed aside the guns he had taken from them. She gave Ki a meaningful glance and then said sharply, "Drop your gun, Bronson. You too, Simpson, Proctor."

The three men stared at her in stunned surprise.

"What the hell—" Bronson began. But he never finished what he had been about to say because Ki shot the gun out of his hand.

A startled Simpson and Proctor quickly dropped their own guns and as quickly raised their hands.

"What is the meaning of this, Jessie?" Bronson barked, no longer startled but now angry, his face reddening and his eyes narrowing as he too raised his hands.

"There'll be no hanging here today," Jessie answered him, her voice blunt.

"No hanging?" blustered Jim Bob Simpson. "These three riders of the long trails—" he glanced at the men who had attempted to rob the stage and who were now under the steady surveillance of Ki's borrowed gun "—they intended to steal the cash box the stage was carrying."

"And rob the passengers too," Charles Proctor added indignantly.

"Maybe even do away with them into the bargain."

"They *deserve* to hang!" Bronson snarled.

"Maybe you're right," Jessie said, "Maybe they do deserve to hang. But you're not going to be the ones to hang them."

"You going to leave us be?" one of the outlaws asked her nervously, his eyes on the black hole in the barrel of the gun in Ki's steady hand.

"You're going to let us go?" piped the man standing next to him.

"Nope," Ki said in answer to both questions.

The two outlaws glared at him.

"Then—what?" one of them asked fearfully.

From the other: "You mean to kill us, is that it?"

"No, that's not it," Ki told them.

"You're going to town," Jessie said. "To the marshal there."

The two outlaws breathed a collective sigh of relief.

Then, as Ki turned, about to say something to Jessie, one of them lunged for the guns Simpson and Proctor had taken from them and tossed on the ground.

"Ki!" Jessie cried in alarm.

162

Before she could say anything more, Ki turned in a swift graceful arc. He tossed his revolver to his left hand. His right slipped into his vest pocket and came out with one of his five-bladed throwing stars. He threw it just as the outlaw came up with the gun he had retrieved from the ground in his hand.

"Owwwww!" the man screamed as the *shuriken* Ki had thrown embedded itself in his hand and the gun he had been holding fell from it. He got a grip on the *shuriken,* cutting his fingers as he did so on the protruding blades of the metal weapon. He let out another howl of pain and then tried again, more gingerly this time, to remove the weapon from his bleeding hand. He succeeded.

"Stand up!" Ki ordered. When the man was on his feet, Ki snapped, "Try a move like that again and my next *shuriken* will kill you. Or maybe I'll use a bullet next time to achieve the same effect."

The cowed gunman stepped back, not even daring to so much as look at the gun he had just dropped as he tightly clutched his wounded hand in an effort to stop its bleeding.

"Jessie," Ki said, without looking at her as he kept his eyes on the outlaws, "I'll take these two into town and turn them over to Marshal Collins. You keep your gun trained on those other three who call themselves vigilantes until I put enough distance between us and them so that they can't catch up with me and take these highwaymen off my hands and hang them. Will you do that?"

"You bet I will."

"Tell that fellow in the frock coat over there that was riding the stage that I'll leave his gun with Marshal Collins," Ki said, and then, to his prisoners, "Get your horses and walk them over to that boulder where I left my mount." He kept his gun trained on them as they retrieved their horses, and then he marched them over to the spot where his horse was lazily munching some browse it had found in the thin shade of a shin oak sapling.

"See you back at the ranch," Jessie called out to him as he swung into the saddle and then, after the outlaws were also aboard their mounts, moved them out.

He waved, acknowledging her words, and minutes later rounded a bend with his prisoners and disappeared from sight.

"I don't know what's got into you, Jessie," Bronson snarled. "Those men should have been strung up. You saw what they did—what they tried to do. They meant to rob the stage and maybe kill its passengers. They did kill the driver and the man who was riding shotgun."

"What's got into me," Jessie said coolly, "is a desire to put a stop to vigilante justice and let the law handle matters such as this."

"The law," Jim Bob Simpson spat contemptuously. "The law'll more'n likely find reasons why those two shouldn't be convicted. Lack of evidence or some such nonsense. It happens all the time. They'll be out again in no time and up to their same nasty shenanigans. Now you tell me if you can, where's the justice in that?"

Jessie didn't deign to answer the question.

"You just might have bitten off more than you can chew, Miss Starbuck," Charles Proctor said. "Maybe you need your head examined going up against the Vigilance Committee like you just did here today."

"Is that a threat, Mr. Proctor? If it is, it doesn't alarm me. I'm perfectly capable of taking care of myself and fending off trouble from whatever quarter it may come—even from the brave but, I submit, badly misguided members of your committee."

Bronson was about to say something when the three men and the lone woman who had been aboard the stage approached and one of the men said, "Miss, I want to thank you and your Oriental friend on behalf of myself and the other passengers for what you just did for us."

"Your friend was really quite magnificent," enthused the woman in the group. "The way he stopped that runaway team—most impressive."

"Thank you," Jessie said. "We were glad to be of help."

"What do you plan to do with these highwaymen?" another of the men asked.

"Wait a minute!" cried the man who had first spoken. "These men aren't the ones who tried to rob us. Why, that's Mr. Simpson and that's Mr. Proctor."

"What is going on here, miss?" the third man in the group asked. "Why are you holding your gun on these three upstanding citizens?"

"Because these upstanding citizens were about to hang those highwaymen," Jessie replied.

For a moment there was stony silence. Then the woman blurted out, "They should have. They most certainly should have rid the earth of such deadly creatures. Why in the world did you stop them from doing so, for heaven's sake?"

"I don't believe in vigilante justice if it means killing unconvicted men," Jessie said sharply. "But I don't intend to go into the matter any further with you. There are things that need doing, and I fully expect you three gentlemen will see to it that they're done since you are all so obviously public-spirited citizens."

"Things?" sniffed the man in the frock coat. "What things?"

"The stage driver and the man riding shotgun with him—their bodies should be taken into town and turned over to the coroner. And the outlaw's too. Since you folks won't be completing your journeys on that stage until a new driver can be provided, why don't you load those two bodies on the stage and take them to town. By the way, sir," she added, addressing the man in the frock coat, "my friend asked me to tell you that you can pick up the gun you loaned him at Marshal Collins's office in town."

There was some grumbling and a few mild protests but, in the end, the three men did, however reluctantly, what Jessie had suggested. By the time they had the bodies loaded onto the stage and the burliest of the three had agreed to act as driver, Jessie decided Ki now had enough of a headstart to town that she could let the three vigilantes go their own ways.

"It's been an interesting meeting, Mel," she said with a smile. "I'll be moving on now, and I expect you and your friends will want to do the same."

"This is not the end of the matter, Jessie," Bronson warned, shaking a finger at her. "You've aligned yourself with the wrong side of the law, and a day of reckoning on that score is bound to come sooner or later, mark my words."

Before Bronson had finished spouting his heated words, Jessie had left him and gone for her horse. She holstered her gun, swung into the saddle, and moved out, heading for home.

★

Chapter 10

Ki received curious stares from people on the street and on the boardwalks in town as he rode behind his two prisoners, gun in hand, heading for the marshal's office.

When he reached it, he ordered the two men he was guarding to dismount. When they had, he did also. Then he marched them into the office.

Marshal Collins looked up from the Montgomery Ward catalog he had been studying as his visitors halted in front of his desk.

"What's this?" he asked.

"Brought you some guests," Ki answered. "These two men just tried to hold up the northbound stage. Miss Starbuck and I stopped them from doing so."

"Well, well, well. Maybe I should deputize you to make this whole thing official."

"No need, Marshal. Just lock these fellows up and bring them before the circuit court judge when he rides in and you'll have done your duty. They killed the driver of the stage and the man on it who was riding shotgun."

Ki placed the gun he was holding on the desk. "That belongs to a fellow wearing a fancy frock coat who was on the stage. I left word for him that he could get his gun back from you."

"What happened to that man's hand?" Collins asked. "You shot him?"

"Nope." Ki took a shiny *shuriken* from his pocket and held it up for the lawman to see. "I used one of these on him. He had taken a notion to ventilate me. I dissuaded him from trying to do so, you might say."

Collins lumbered to his feet and took down a ring of keys that had been hanging on a nail driven into the wall behind his desk. "Let's go, boys."

When he had the two men locked up in a cell in the rear of his office, he returned and sat down at his desk again. "I reckon I ought to thank you for what you did, you and Miss Starbuck."

"It would be nice to hear some thanks. We sure didn't get any from Mel Bronson and his friends, who rode up on the attempted robbery."

"Mr. Bronson was at the scene?"

"Him and Mr. Simpson and Mr. Proctor, yes. They were also involved in shooting it out with those failed highwaymen I brought you. They intended to hang them once the shooting ended. We stopped them from doing so."

"I'll bet that didn't set easy with Mr. Bronson, now, did it?"

"When I left him, he was one unhappy man. Acted, he did, like a kid whose favorite toy was taken away from him."

"I'd like to make a suggestion, if it won't make your fur fly."

"Suggest away, Marshal."

"I'd suggest you—Miss Starbuck too—would be smart to steer clear of Mel Bronson and his vigilantes after what you tell me you both just did. He's not the type to take kindly to anybody who interferes in his plans, and it appears you two did just that."

"Be seeing you, Marshal," Ki said before turning on his heels and leaving the office.

● ● ●

Jessie had been home for only a short while when a knock sounded on the front door. She opened it and found, to her great surprise, Evelyn Pruitt standing outside, her buggy parked not far away.

"Evelyn, come in. You look upset. What is it? What's wrong?"

Evelyn didn't answer until she was inside the house and Jessie had taken her by the arm and led her to a chair. Then, as she sat down in the chair and looked up at Jessie with a beseeching expression on her pale face, she said, "I lied to you."

"Lied to me? About what?" The words were no sooner out of her mouth than Jessie was sure she knew what Evelyn was referring to. "You mean about Moses Slater? About having been raped by him?"

The muscles in Evelyn's face grew taut. She nodded, her eyes pleading. For what, Jessie wondered. Forgiveness? Understanding?

Jessie sat down opposite Evelyn. "Tell me what really happened."

Evelyn drew a deep breath and then let it out. Looking down at her hands, which were clenched in her lap, she began. "Mr. Bronson visited me quite unexpectedly. Daddy wasn't home at the time. I invited him in and asked him it he would like some coffee or something stronger perhaps. He said no, he had no time for the amenities. He had come, he said, on business. Important business."

Jessie wished Evelyn would quickly get to the point, but she decided against urging her to do so. She was afraid the woman would bolt if she did. Or break into tears. Evelyn seemed on the verge of becoming distraught. At the breaking point.

"I couldn't imagine what Mr. Bronson meant. I mean about having come about important business. Did I tell you that Daddy was not at home at the time?" When Jessie nodded, Evelyn continued. "I couldn't imagine what business Mr. Bronson could possibly have with me."

"What business *did* he have with you?"

"He asked me if I knew that he held a chattel mortgage on Daddy's cattle, and I told him yes, I did. He asked me if I knew what would happen if he should decide to demand full payment of that mortgage. I said I did—that Daddy would lose his cattle because I was sure he could not possibly pay off the mortgage all at one time. I begged him not to do it.

"He said he had no intention of doing such a thing. I was so relieved, I can't tell you. But then he said he had no intention of doing so if I cooperated with him. That's the way he put it. If I 'cooperated' with him. He proceeded to tell me what he meant by that."

Evelyn squeezed her eyes shut. Tears oozed out of them onto her cheeks. With her eyes still closed, she said, "He told me if I wanted to protect Daddy, I would say that Moses Slater raped me. I couldn't believe I had heard him correctly. When I said something to that effect, he restated what he wanted me to do in no uncertain terms just as he had the first time. When I asked him why he wanted me to make such a false accusation against an innocent man, he told me that was none of my business. I was not, he said, to ask questions. I told him I could not possibly do what he wished. He reminded me then that Daddy would be ruined if I refused. I was in a terrible quandary. My mind seemed to be on fire. He pressed me for an answer. He said if I were to tell anyone what he had asked of me, he would deny it. He said no one would believe such a wild story. I thought at the time that was probably true. I thought of Daddy and what would happen if I didn't go along with Mr. Bronson. Finally, I said—I said I would do it."

"And you did it. You claimed that Moses Slater had raped you."

"Yes," she said softly.

Jessie's mind was racing. Forcing herself to remain calm, she asked, "Would you be willing to testify in court about what you just told me? Would you tell a judge and jury what you just told me?"

As Evelyn hesitated, Jessie held her breath, knowing how much depended upon the woman's answer to her question.

170

"Yes."

The word, that one single word, made Jessie want to jump for joy. She had to force herself to remain seated and to speak in a normal voice.

"Evelyn, I want you to stay here. I have to leave but you must stay."

"Stay here? But, Jessie, why?"

"You'll be safe here. Safe from Mel Bronson," she added in a meaningful tone.

Evelyn's eyes widened as she stared at Jessie. "Do you think he would try to harm me?"

"I think he might, yes."

Evelyn's face grew even paler.

"But don't worry. Ki will be home soon. When he gets here, tell him what you just told me. He'll protect you if anything untoward should happen. I'm going to see Marshal Collins. I'm going to tell him what you told me. I'm going to ask him to look into the circumstances of Moses Slater's death more carefully. I'm going to tell him that I think Mel Bronson arranged to have Moses Slater killed by the vigilantes to benefit himself."

"I don't understand."

"Neither do I, to be truthful about it. But I suspect that Mel Bronson set his vigilantes on Moses Slater to cover up something, something that Moses Slater knew which might harm Bronson."

"But what could that possibly be?"

Again Jessie had to admit that she hadn't the faintest idea. "But Bronson must have wanted Moses Slater out of the way, so he conceived the cock-and-bull story that he then blackmailed you into telling."

"I'm so ashamed of the terrible thing I did. But, Jessie, I was so fearful of what would happen to Daddy—to both of us if I didn't do what Mr. Bronson wanted."

"What you did was a very grave mistake, Evelyn, I can't deny that. It cost an innocent man his life. But now you have told the truth. Only a brave woman, a woman of conscience, would have done such a thing."

Evelyn's face regained some of its normal color. The frantic look began to leave her eyes. She came close to smiling, but smiling, for Evelyn Pruitt, Jessie believed, was still some time away.

"I'm going into town now to see Marshal Collins," she announced, rising. "But first, I'm going to call on Mel Bronson and tell him I know what he forced you to do even if I don't know why he forced you to do it."

"You had better be careful, Jessie," Evelyn declared. "I'm convinced Mr. Bronson is a dangerous man."

"So am I," were Jessie's parting words.

As Ki opened the door of the house and stepped inside, he stopped in his tracks and stared at Evelyn Pruitt, who was standing beside one of the windows and looking out.

She turned and smiled when she saw him. "I'm—"

"I know who you are," he interrupted. "We met at the corn husking last fall. You're Evelyn Pruitt, a friend of Jessie's."

"I'd forgotten that we had met. Of course, I knew who you were. Everyone in town does. How are you, Ki?"

"I'm fine. Where's Jessie?"

"She's gone to town. She asked me to remain here and tell you—"

"Gone to town? That's strange. She would have just gotten home from town not long ago. Why did she decide to go back?"

"If you'll let me, I'll explain," Evelyn said a bit testily as she moved away from the window and into the center of the room. "I came here to tell her that I had lied to her— to everyone—about being raped by Moses Slater."

Ki's eyes narrowed as he studied Evelyn's face.

"I just couldn't stand myself for telling such a terrible falsehood. Nor could I live any longer with the knowledge that I was responsible, in a way, for Mr. Slater's death.

"Anyway, I came here this afternoon and I told Jessie the truth. That I wasn't raped. That Mr. Bronson blackmailed me into lying by threatening my daddy."

"Why did he do that?"

172

"I don't know. I told Jessie I didn't. She thinks there must have been a reason why Mr. Bronson wanted Mr. Slater dead. When I was forced to make my accusation against him, which I assure you I shall regret until my dying day, he then rode out with his vigilantes and caught and hanged Mr. Slater for a crime he never committed. Jessie was absolutely incensed when she learned that Mr. Slater was innocent."

"She never for a minute believed he was guilty."

"Well, now she's gone to town, and she told me to tell you that she was going straight to Marshal Collins to tell him what I told her this afternoon—the truth. No, that's wrong."

"What's wrong?"

"She's not going straight to Marshal Collins. She said she was going to call first on Mr. Bronson and tell him what I told her. She was, I suspect, going to see if she could find out why Mr. Bronson made me tell that horrible untruth I did."

Ki groaned inwardly. The thought of Jessie confronting Bronson with her newly gained—and very definitely dangerous—knowledge sent a chill coursing through him.

"Where are you going?" Evelyn asked him.

"I'm going to town."

"Why?"

"I'm worried about Jessie. I don't think she should have decided to confront Bronson with what she found out from you. There's no telling what he's liable to do once he knows that you've let the cat out of the bag and that she intends to take that cat to the law."

"Oh, I wish I had never heard of Mr. Mel Bronson!" Evelyn wailed. "He has ruined my life! Simply *ruined* it!"

Ki left the house and climbed aboard his horse. He wheeled his mount and went galloping toward town.

"I know what you did, Mel," Jessie told Bronson as she stood in front of the desk in his office. "You murdered Moses Slater."

Bronson stared at her in amazement, his eyebrows rising in a show of skepticism that bordered on scorn. "Jessie, I

173

always considered you to be a sane and sensible woman, but here you are accusing me of murder, which is about the most preposterous thing I ever have heard of."

"I don't find it preposterous at all. Not in the least. I have proof."

"Oh, ho! You have proof. What kind of proof is it that you think you have against me?"

"The words of Evelyn Pruitt, that's what."

Bronson's eyebrows collapsed and his face darkened. He leaned forward in his chair, one large hand twisting a large glass paperweight in a tightly confined circle. "What in the world has Evelyn Pruitt to do with this bizarre story of yours?"

"In a nutshell—everything. Evelyn told me after I left you and your two companions that you blackmailed her into accusing Moses Slater of having raped her."

"Ridiculous!" Bronson spluttered.

"She said you visited her and threatened to ruin her father if she didn't cooperate with you."

"Nonsense!" Bronson bellowed, punctuating the word by picking up and then slamming down the paperweight in his hand.

"When she had done what you demanded of her, you rounded up your vigilantes and went after Moses. You caught him and you hanged him for a crime he never committed."

Bronson relaxed. He put down the paperweight and leaned back in his chair. He stared up at Jessie, an almost placid expression on his face.

"Evelyn Pruitt is a liar," he said. "What's more, she may very well be mentally deranged as a result of her ordeal at the hands of that animal Slater. Imagine her making a charge of such a farfetched nature against me, a respectable businessman and staunch pillar, if I do say so myself, of this town's society."

"I don't think Evelyn is lying. I think she told me the truth."

"What happened to her has apparently unbalanced her mind."

"I knew from the beginning that Moses Slater was not the kind of man to commit any lawless act. He certainly would never have committed an act so brutal, so unspeakable, as rape. Evelyn has now come forward to confirm my judgment."

"Who do you think will believe her?"

"A judge. A jury."

Bronson leaned forward again. "She's going to carry this to the extreme of a trial?"

"She is, yes. With my wholehearted support and encouragement."

"I'll fight her and I'll fight you. I'll see you both in hell before I'll let you crazy females intimidate me!"

Bronson paused for a moment and then, beginning to grin, said, "You say I murdered Moses Slater—that is, Evelyn Pruitt says so."

"You did, with the help of your vigilantes."

"Then tell me this if you can. Why would I do such a thing?"

Jessie hesitated. Bronson had her and she knew it. She had been expecting his question, and now that it had come she didn't know how to answer it. Finally, she forced herself to say, "I don't know."

"There, you see?" Bronson shot to his feet. He shook a finger at Jessie. "I had no more reason to murder Moses Slater than I did to murder the man in the moon."

"You had a reason. I just don't know at this moment what that reason was. But you did have one, I'm sure of that. I'm going now to Marshal Collins, and I'm going to tell him what Evelyn Pruitt told me, and I'm also going to tell him that she will testify against you at your trial. Maybe during the trial we'll discover your motive for murdering Moses."

As Jessie turned and started for the door, Bronson yelled after her, "Damn you, Jessie Starbuck. You are nothing but an interfering bitch!"

Jessie paid him no attention as she reached for the doorknob.

But when she heard the sound of hurried footsteps behind her, she started to turn. But it was already too late. The heavy glass paperweight in Bronson's hand struck her on the back of the head, and she was plunged instantly into an ocean of utter darkness.

Ki burst into Marshal Collins' office, which was occupied by the marshal and two men whom Ki recognized as vigilantes—Charles Proctor and Jim Bob Simpson.

"I'm looking for Jessie Starbuck," Ki said. "Has she been here?"

The marshal held up a hand to silence him and continued talking to the two vigilantes facing his desk. "Like I said, Whit Price is off an another bender and this time he's finished. I've fired him. Cy Walker, my other deputy, quit on me yesterday, so if you two want to be deputies all you've got to do is say the word."

Before either man could speak, Ki pushed them aside and asked, "Has Jessie Starbuck been here?"

"Yes, she's been here," an annoyed Collins responded.

"How long ago?"

"You mean how long ago today?"

"Yes, dammit!"

"I never said she was here *today*."

Simpson and Proctor joined in Collins's mocking laughter.

Ki ignored them. "She's not been to see you today then?"

"Nope. Was she fixing to come here today?"

"She was—to tell you that Mel Bronson and some of his vigilantes hanged Moses Slater when he wasn't guilty of raping Evelyn Pruitt as she charged. Jessie was also going to confront and accuse Bronson of having hanged an innocent man for some reason known only to him."

The other three men in the room exchanged startled glances.

"What I've told you—it's true. Evelyn Pruitt confessed to Jessie and to me too that she was forced by Bronson to tell that rape story of hers. I think Jessie never should have gone near him. If she did, I think she might be in danger. But if Bronson harms so much as a hair on her head, I'll kill him."

"Now you hold on one minute, mister!" Collins said, springing to his feet. "You'd best not try anything like that or I'll put you in a cell and keep you there so long you'll rot."

Ki, at the door, turned and said, "You heard me, Marshal. I'm going to kill Bronson if he's harmed Jessie in any way. If you think you're man enough to stop me, you're welcome to try."

As Ki went through the door, he heard Collins say, "So speak up, you two. Are you going to let me deputize you or do I have to go after that man myself before he does Mel Bronson in?"

Ki slammed the door behind him and ran down the street, leaving his horse tied to the hitch rail in front of the marshal's office. When he reached Bronson's office, he tried the door and found it locked. He hammered hard on it, but got no response. He tried to peer around the edges of the green shade that was drawn down over the glass in the door, but he could see nothing and no one inside.

A grizzled old man seated in a rickety rocking chair that creaked as it rocked back and forth on its runners drawled, "You're too late, if it's Mr. Bronson you be seeking."

"He's not in his office?"

"Nope. Left town, he did, awhile ago. Must have been in a helluva hurry, him and the woman he had with him."

"Woman. What woman?"

"Now how would I know what woman?"

"Did she have hair the color of copper, by any chance?"

The man took a pipe from his mouth, grinned, and jabbed its stem in Ki's direction. "Be she the one you're really after? She was pretty, she was, though she was soused."

"Soused? What do you mean?"

"She was passed out. Couldn't walk. Bronson had to practically carry her to his buggy."

Jessie? Soused? Ki didn't believe it for a minute. "Which way did they go?"

"West."

Ki thanked the man and raced back to the horse. He freed it from the hitch rail, looped the reins over the

177

animal's head, swung into the saddle, and rode out of town, heading west.

He scanned the road he was traveling, and finally was able to make out the fresh ruts left by a buggy and the team pulling it that practically obliterated other older tracks. He followed the hot trail until he came to a place where the buggy had left the road and headed northwest through some tall wheat grass. Now the trail was even easier to follow because the grass had been crushed down and had not yet had time to spring back.

Sometime later, he spotted the buggy up ahead of him in the distance. It was rocking slightly as if about to lose a wheel. He spurred his horse and drew closer to it. He had almost reached it when he saw Jessie leap from the vehicle's passenger seat and begin to run through the tall grass that hid the lower half of her body from sight. An instant later, a shot rang out. Jessie disappeared from sight.

Ki's heart froze.

Bronson leaped from the buggy and went running toward the spot where Jessie had disappeared from sight.

Ki wheeled his horse and set out after Bronson. He cut the man off just as Jessie, to Ki's immense relief, stood up in the ocean of grass.

Bronson turned, raised the gun in his hand, and took aim at Ki. The round he fired went over Ki's head. He was about to fire again when three men rode into view.

"Hold it right there!" Marshal Collins barked as he drew rein and leveled his gun at Ki. Beside him, wearing tin badges, were Jim Bob Simpson and Charles Proctor.

"That man just tried to kill me with his bare hands!" Bronson yelled at the top of his voice and pointed to Ki. "And she *kidnapped* me!"

"I did no such thing!" Jessie exclaimed at the same time that Ki said, "He's lying!"

"She came to my office and pulled a gun on me and forced me to drive out here!" Bronson persisted. "Marshal, she was going to kill me. Then her partner in crime there, he arrived on the scene and he attacked me."

"I'll lock them both up until such time as we can sort all this out, Mr. Bronson," Collins declared decisively. "Let's go, you two. You're going to jail, both of you."

"Mel Bronson murdered Moses Slater with the help of his vigilantes," Jessie said, her voice rising.

"Your friend said something about that when he came by my office looking for you," Collins mused, stroking his chin and giving Bronson a speculative glance. "Something about Evelyn Pruitt saying she was never raped by Slater in the first place."

"That's right, Marshal," Jessie said, suddenly encouraged by Collins's hesitancy. "She never was." She explained in a rush what Evelyn Pruitt had told her about Bronson.

When she had finished doing so, Collins said, "Maybe I ought to have me a long talk with this Pruitt woman."

Bronson laughed heartily. Then, with a dismissive wave of his hand, he said, "There's absolutely no need to, Marshal. The Pruitt woman must be hysterical. What reason would I have to force her, as she now chooses to claim I did, to lie about Moses Slater? As for this Starbuck woman, for her to say, as she just now so boldly has, that I wanted Moses Slater dead—again without any sort of substantiation for her claim—it's outrageous!"

"Well, Mr. Bronson, you may have a point there," Collins drawled.

"Of course I have. What you've just been hearing today are the rantings of unhinged women. Now I insist that you take these two vandals to jail before they try again to do me harm."

"Marshal," Jessie pleaded, "Moses Slater was a kind and gentle man. He wouldn't hurt a fly. Why, when I was a child, he and I would take long rides together and he never ever acted out of line in any way with me. He . . ."

Jessie suddenly fell silent. Her brow furrowed thoughtfully.

Ki glanced at her, waiting for her to go on, wondering what was going through her mind. Clearly something was.

"Marshal, I would like to ask a favor of you," she said finally.

Collins frowned.

"On our way back to town, could we stop by Big Bend?"

The marshal hesitated only a moment before answering, "I don't see why not. Let's go."

Moments later they were all riding out, Jessie seated behind Ki on his horse. When they neared the crossroads at Big Bend, Jessie suddenly slid down over the rump of Ki's horse and went running toward the tall pine tree that grew there.

"Stop her, Marshal!" Bronson screamed from his buggy. "She's getting away!"

Collins promptly galloped after Jessie while the two deputized vigilantes remained where they were, their guns trained on Ki.

Jessie arrived at the pine tree and immediately fell on her knees beside it. She felt about among the creepers covering its trunk, and soon found what she had been searching for. She thrust her hand into the hole in the tree's trunk where she had left so many "secret" messages for Moses Slater when she was a child, and where he had left as many, if not more, for her. When her hand emerged from the hole it held a folded piece of paper. As Collins rode up and drew rein, she unfolded the paper and quickly read the words scrawled in pencil on it.

Then she looked up at Collins, a look of triumph on her face. She stood up and handed him the paper. "Read this, Marshal."

Collins had just finished reading the note when the others arrived on the scene.

"Well, I'll be damned and then double-damned!" he exclaimed in an awed tone.

Which caused Proctor to ask, "What's going on, Marshal?"

"This here note was written by Moses Slater and hid in a hole in that there tree. It says he saw Mel Bronson steal Sid Blanton's horse, Champion, and then put him in Bob Warner's barn under cover of darkness."

"Let me see that note," Simpson said, holding out his hand.

Collins handed it to him. "It also says that Slater went to Miss Starbuck to tell her about what he'd seen, but it seems he missed her. He then went to Bronson and told him he'd seen Bronson steal the horse, and he told him too that he was going to the law about it."

"But he never had the chance," Jessie declared sadly. "One of Mel's vigilantes caught up with him at Big Bend and they hanged him after ransacking his house for some reason or other."

"You knew this note was here?" Collins inquired.

Jessie shook her head. "I was thinking about finding Moses's body as we started back to town. I was thinking that the man had died unnecessarily for a crime he never committed. I was recalling how Moses and I used to leave notes for one another in the hole in that pine tree when I was just a child. It was a sort of game we used to play. It suddenly struck me that maybe Moses might have left me one last note to tell me what he had come to my home to tell me when I wasn't there."

"He must have written this knowing he was going to die," Proctor said after he too had read the note and handed it back to Collins.

"I'm sure he did," Jessie stated. "As such then, it's what I've heard called a dying declaration."

"Which means?" Simpson prompted.

"That Slater can be safely assumed to have told the truth in it," Jessie explained. "No man who knows he is about to die, the law believes, will lie. I'm sure beyond the faintest shadow of a doubt that Moses did not in his note."

Everyone turned to stare at Bronson, who sat in his buggy fidgeting with the reins. "I deny everything," he snapped.

"You can do your denying before a judge," Collins told him bluntly.

Jessie walked over to the buggy. "What were you and the others looking for in Moses's house that you ransacked?" she asked him.

Before he could answer, Charles Proctor spoke up. "I was on that hunt for Slater, Miss Starbuck. None of us ransacked Slater's house. I'll swear on my deathbed to that."

Jessie looked from Bronson to Proctor and then back again as an idea occurred to her. "It was you who ransacked the house, wasn't it, Mel?" As Bronson stated stony-eyed at her, she continued. "You went back after the hanging without any of your friends and went through the house. You were looking for the diamond ring that belonged to Moses. The one he had given to a girl many years ago and got back when she jilted him. He must have told everyone within miles of here about that ring. He called it a sign of his youthful folly, and claimed he kept it to remind him not to be so foolish again in affairs of the heart."

"Let's ride," Collins said gruffly. "The sooner we get this gent—" he nodded at Bronson "—under lock and key the better off we'll all be."

As the mounted men started to move out, Bronson suddenly reached out and seized Jessie. He dragged her into his buggy and wrapped his right forearm around her neck.

"*You* ride out!" he screamed at the others. "*I've* got other plans. Don't any of you try to make a move on me. If you do, I'll shoot her."

His gun was out again and its barrel was pressing against Jessie's temple.

Ki sat his saddle, his hands stiff on his saddlehorn as he watched the fear flare in his friend's eyes.

"What she said, it's all true, isn't it, Bronson?" Collins asked.

"It is," the man admitted almost boastfully. "The lady's not only clever, she's also lucky. I intended to kill her somewhere out here and leave her body to be found after she came to me and told me Evelyn Pruitt had turned against me and she was going to tell you what I'd made her do. It would have been considered a killing by person or persons unknown. No one ever would have suspected me. Not once I'd got my hands on Evelyn Pruitt and killed her too."

"So you'd be safe," Collins prompted.

Bronson nodded.

"I would have hounded you until the truth came out," Ki said. "Evelyn Pruitt also told me what she told Jessie."

"If you did that," Bronson snarled, "you'd have wound up as dead as the two women."

"Why'd you steal Blanton's horse and put it in Bob Warner's barn?" Simpson asked Bronson.

"To get my hands on the Warner land. They had water and they wouldn't let me use it. We'd had a dispute some time ago, so they kept me away from that water. Well, they overstepped themselves, they did, when they tried to outfox me. Once Warner had been hanged for horse thievery, I went ahead and bought Warner's land through a holding company I control. I knew the Widow Warner wouldn't be able to hang onto it. They were too deep in debt for that. So once I'd arranged to have Warner hanged for supposedly stealing Blanton's horse, the coast, as they say, was clear."

Simpson swore colorfully.

"What about that young fellow, Jerry Talbot?" Proctor asked. "Did he really kill Denby like he said he was going to do?"

Bronson's lips twisted in a sneer. "He didn't kill Denby. I did."

Proctor gasped and asked, "Why?"

"Why?" Bronson's sneer was full-blown now. "Jerry Talbot and I both wanted the same woman—Janice Drake. She was leaning in his favor. So I got him hanged for supposedly murdering Denby, and now Janice and I are going to get married.

"By the way," Bronson continued coolly, "the lady here was right about the Slater diamond. I went back on my own to his house and searched for the ring like she said. I searched the place and I found it. Once I sell that diamond, the cash it'll bring will make a nice nest egg for me and Janice Drake to start our married life together with."

"You'll never marry her or anybody else," Collins muttered. "Not where you're going."

"You're wrong about that, Marshal. Because I'm not going to jail. I'm going to get Janice Drake and we're leaving here for parts unknown. You'll never see either of us again. If any of you tries anything stupid, you'll never see Jessie Starbuck again either—not alive, that is. Now I'm going to drive away from here and you are all going to stay right where you are. You got that, Marshal?"

Collins hesitated and then, with obvious reluctance, nodded.

Bronson put his gun down on the seat beside him. Keeping a tight hold on Jessie's throat with his forearm, he reached for the reins.

But Jessie beat him to it. She reached out, seized the reins, and violently slapped the rump of Bronson's horse with them. As the horse bolted, she reached up and seized Bronson's arm that was around her throat as he, knocked off balance by the bolting team, fought to maintain his hold on her.

She tore his arm away from her throat and then grabbed the side of the buggy, prepared to vault to the ground. But before she could do so, Bronson retrieved his gun and was about to fire it at her.

Ki ripped a throwing star from his vest pocket and hurled it at Bronson. The five-bladed metal *shuriken* bit into Bronson's forehead and then into his brain, killing him almost instantly.

Jessie sprang from the coach and ran to Ki. He dismounted, took her in his arms, and held her close as she shivered while fighting to regain control of herself.

"That's it," Collins said. "It's finished."

There was silence for a moment until Proctor broke it by saying, "So are the vigilantes."

"A good thing," Jessie said, "if you ask me." She left the shelter of Ki's embrace and turned to face the other men. "We never should have formed the Vigilance Committee in the first place," she added firmly.

"We did some good," Jim Bob Simpson ventured. "Those rustlers . . ."

"They were caught in the act of stealing stock," Proctor pointed out.

"They all should have been turned over to Marshal Collins," Jessie said. "It wasn't your job or my job to find them guilty. Nor was it our job to pass sentence on and execute them. If we turn our backs on the law, even in the name of justice, we turn our backs on everything good and just that holds us together as a civilized society."

"Amen," Marshal Collins said.

Jessie and Ki watched the three men move out then as they rode toward town, Proctor driving Bronson's buggy, its owner's lifeless body slumped on the seat beside him.

"*Requiescat in pace*," Ki said softly.

Jessie glanced at him.

"That means, 'Rest in peace.' Maybe Moses Slater, Bob Warner, and Jerry Talbot can now rest in peace, I mean."

Jessie took his offered hand and, with his help, climbed behind him. They rode out, heading home, as the sun was setting on a day neither of them was sorry to see end.